How to Propose to a Princess

—

Rebecca Winters

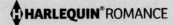

HARLEQUIN®ROMANCE

Recycling programs
for this product may
not exist in your area.

ISBN-13: 978-1-335-49955-4

How to Propose to a Princess

First North American publication 2019

HARLEQUIN®

www.Harlequin.com

Printed in U.S.A.

Rebecca Winters lives in Salt Lake City, Utah. With canyons and high alpine meadows full of wildflowers, she never runs out of places to explore. They, plus her favorite vacation spots in Europe, often end up as backgrounds for her romance novels—because writing is her passion, along with her family and church. Rebecca loves to hear from readers. If you wish to email her, please visit her website at rebeccawinters.net.

Books by Rebecca Winters

Harlequin Romance

Visit the Author Profile page at Harlequin.com for more titles.

To my dear daughter Dominique, herself a wonderful writer, who cried through parts of this story with me. That told me her heart had been touched, too.

Praise for
Rebecca Winters

"Readers will be swept away.... Winters' fine romance unfolds at the perfect pace, so one can digest the relationship and still enjoy the antics of being a billionaire."

—*RT Book Reviews* on *The Billionaire Who Saw Her Beauty*

CHAPTER ONE

THOUGH OFFICE HOURS for patients ended at four thirty p.m. weekdays, and the receptionist had gone, Dr. Nico Barsotti didn't say good-night to his last patient until five thirty Tuesday evening. Even after diagnosing her with strep throat and writing out a prescription, he still couldn't call it a night. Before he could grab a bite in town on his way home, he needed to check on his nine-year-old patient, Tommaso Coletti.

Once he'd said good-night to his nurse who would lock up, he walked through the Hospital of the Three Crosses in the capital city of Domodossola to the pediatric floor in the other wing. The boy had suffered a ruptured appendix on Monday evening. Dr. Sala had performed the surgery, but Nico was his physician. He needed to follow up on the course of IV antibiotics he'd ordered and study the latest lab tests.

Nico nodded to the charting nurse at the station before walking into the room. He'd expected to see at least one of the boy's parents. Instead he beheld a sight that brought him to a halt.

Sitting in a chair next to the bed reading to him was a woman probably in her midtwenties who had luminous golden hair that fell to her shoulders. She wore a light blue volunteer lab coat over a dark blue dress. He caught a glimpse of her lovely profile and moved closer to discover she was reading a book popular with children.

Adriano, il Cane di Pompei was the story of a special stray dog who saw ancient Pompei as a magical place with its archaeological sites. The smile on Tommaso's face meant he was enjoying it. Who wouldn't be mesmerized by the woman's voice? She read it with all the charm and allure of a great storyteller.

He waited until she'd finished before walking over to the other side of the bed. His gaze met hers. Between her light sea glass blue eyes and golden hair, he couldn't look anywhere else. Nico knew he'd seen that beautiful face before. But where?

The blonde knockout reminded him of a celebrity, but he couldn't think which one. She gave him an enticing smile she probably wasn't aware of. That's when he remembered. Last month she'd been eating in the hospital cafeteria with Mia Giancarlo, one of the nurses. He recalled she'd been wearing a silky print blouse and skirt, her womanly figure transformed. Her image had stayed in his mind, and he'd been looking for her ever since.

"Look who's here, Tommaso," she said. "It's Dr. Barsotti."

The boy turned his head in Nico's direction, his eyes excited. *"Dottore—"*

"Ehi, Tommaso. I can see you've been well entertained. *Come stai?"*

"Fausta has been reading to me!"

Fausta? The name rang a bell.

Santo cielo! Now it was all coming back to him. *Princess Fausta Rossiano in the flesh.*

"How do you do, Princess?" he said as he checked the IV bag and took Tommaso's vital signs. "He's a lucky boy to receive a visit from you."

"I'm the lucky one, *dottore."*

"Her name's Fausta," Tommaso corrected him.

Nico smiled to himself.

The three daughters of King Victor, ruler of the small country of Domodossola that touched on the borders of France, Switzerland and Italy, were known for their beauty. During these last few years there'd been two royal marriages, and their pictures had been on TV and in the newspaper. Nico ought to know since the magazines in his office put there for the patients were filled with royal news. There'd been constant speculation that the third stunning princess would be marrying a royal prince in the near future.

He shouldn't be surprised that the yet unmarried daughter of the royal family would actually volunteer her time this way. They did a lot of admirable philanthropy for the country. Her friendliness had won over his patient.

"When can I go home?"

"You're doing much better this evening, Tommaso. I'll probably release you in the morning." He turned to put some information into the computer.

"Not until then?" the boy muttered. "I'm fine now."

"We must do what Dr. Barsotti says!"

Tommaso's father had arrived. His wife followed him inside. Nico watched their interaction. Tommaso didn't know how lucky he was to have loving parents. Nico had grown up in an orphanage run by the nuns. For years he'd been trying to find his parents and where he'd come from with no success.

After they thanked the princess for her time, she slipped quietly from the room. He gave instructions to the parents before he left to catch up with her. Strongly drawn to her by her appeal, he wanted to get acquainted, but other than staff, he saw no sign of her in the corridor.

He approached the charge nurse. "When did Princess Fausta start reading to the children?"

The other woman's face broke into a broad smile. "She's been a hospital volunteer for several months in the geriatric department. This week she was assigned to Pediatrics. So far, all the patients have been delighted. She has a real way with them. We're excited she'll be working with us until she's transferred to another department."

"When will she be here again?"

"Tomorrow. For the time being she comes on the afternoon shift four times a week."

"I see. Thank you."

Nico left the hospital, glad he had to wait

only until tomorrow when he checked on another patient. Hopefully he'd find her here.

During the drive back to the palace in the limo, Fausta relived those moments in Tommaso's hospital room when Dr. Barsotti had come in. Over the past two months she'd seen him several times from a distance when he'd come in to the hospital cafeteria. But they hadn't actually spoken to each other until now.

Fausta hadn't thought it possible to be attracted to another man after her heart had been broken four years ago. Dego Spinella had been her childhood sweetheart.

Dego's father, Tano, had been the personal chauffeur for her father over the years. He, along with his wife and two children, lived in a house on the estate. Their son Dego was Fausta's age. Along with her sisters, they'd all played outside together over the years. As they grew older, the friendship between Fausta and Dego grew into love.

They'd planned to go to the University of Domodossola together and then get married. But her dream was shattered when one day just before college started, her father told her that Dego was leaving for Rome, Italy, to attend college there. The king had made plans to pay for his lodging and tuition as his way of thanking Tano and their family for all their years of service.

In panic, Fausta had phoned Dego. "Why didn't you refuse my father so we could be together?" she cried in despair. "That's all you had to do!"

"How could I turn down his kindness, Fausta? As Papa said, this is a once in a lifetime opportunity for me. Our family doesn't have that kind of money. But you and I will phone and send letters. After graduation we'll be together again and make plans for our future."

What future? You've stabbed my heart, Dego.

Fausta's father hadn't forced him to go. It had all been up to Dego, but he hadn't fought for their love.

"Cara?" he'd prodded when she hadn't answered. "Tell me you understand. Of course I love you and am going to miss you, but he's been so good to our family and he *is* the king."

That's right, and she'd been born the daughter of a king instead of a commoner like she'd wanted to be. "I understand more than you think."

Fausta had never liked being royal and her parents knew it, but the years growing up around Dego had been idyllic. He wasn't royal and they got along so perfectly, she knew a marriage between them would end in a lasting love match. Her plans for them to get a little home in the city where they could raise a family and live a normal life with children had been her dream.

But his willingness to leave her without begging her to go to Rome with him was worse than a betrayal. She'd thought their love had meant everything to him, but nothing could have been further from the truth. Fausta had been living in a fantasy world with no substance. Many times they'd come close to making love but had decided to wait until they were engaged.

His sudden departure had left her feeling heartbroken and betrayed. Her father had known she was in love with Dego and she knew he didn't like it. But he wouldn't have stood in the way of her marrying *if* Dego had loved her enough.

The fact that Dego had left for Rome without agonizing over them being torn apart said it all. The phone calls and letters from him came less and less, killing her feelings. In time she learned he'd married an Italian girl. Dego had been subtly bribed, and more than ever she hated that she'd been born a royal.

In the last four years there'd been no other man. She knew her parents were hoping she'd end up marrying one of the princes on their short list. But that would *never* happen! *One day she'd find herself a commoner who couldn't be bought for any reason!*

Her thoughts flashed back to Dr. Barsotti.

The second she'd laid eyes on the family practice doctor with his dark fringed midnight blue eyes and black-brown hair, his image had filled her thoughts. At six foot three with a rock-solid physique and potently male, no other man could come close to him.

Just hearing about his virtues from her best friend, Mia, revealed qualities beyond his looks. Besides being twenty-eight and single, he wasn't a baron, a count, a duke or a prince. Pure and simple, he was a nonroyal doctor, already a revered professional who she doubted could be intimidated, manipulated or bought at any price.

Once in her apartment at the palace, she phoned Mia because she'd promised.

"Fausta? I've been waiting to hear from you."

"I just barely got home from the hospital after my first shift on the pediatric ward. It was so much fun."

"I know how much you love kids."

"I do." Fausta adored children and looked forward to the day when she had a family of her own and an attentive husband who had no other duties than to come home at the end of the day and be with them.

"Any sightings of Dr. Barsotti?"

She gripped her cell phone tighter. "He came in to check on one of his patients while I was reading to Tommaso."

"How did that go? I guess the doctor went into shock to see Princess Fausta Rossiano working there."

Fausta's breath caught. "I hope it was a good one."

A small laugh escaped her friend's lips. "Do you honestly know a man who wouldn't be thrilled to get near you if he could?"

"*Mia—*"

"Stop pretending when you know it's true."

"The good doctor didn't seem to care that I left the room. I could have been wearing a quarantine sign for his lack of interest."

"Don't be ridiculous. You're the daughter of King Victor, *that's* why he played it cool. He doesn't want to presume. Felipe is the same way when it comes to you."

"I know." Dr. Felipe Peletti, a friend of Dr. Barsotti's in the same medical group, had been dating Mia. The two were in love. "There are certain lines they won't cross."

"I'm afraid most ordinary people, men in particular, have the same problem when it comes to your *royalness*," Mia teased.

Fausta's friend had never had that hang-up. They'd met in high school with no secrets between them. She was one of the few nonroyals who'd treated them like equals and Fausta loved her for it. "You mean my *untouchableness*."

"If only the masses knew what a fun, easy person you are to be with."

"Ditto. Now I'd better let you go. I know you have to be at the hospital first thing in the morning. See you for lunch at Babbo's." It was a trattoria around the corner from the hospital.

"Absolutely."

"Ciao."

Wednesday after office hours, Nico was elated to find the princess comforting his ten-year-old patient Gina. The girl suffered from a form of childhood absence epilepsy. Each seizure lasted ten to twenty seconds and ended abruptly. Two out of three children responded to treatment and the seizures usually disappeared by midadolescence.

He'd had her brought in for tests before he ordered medication for her. She was holding on to a new stuffed animal for dear life.

The princess looked up at him when he entered the room. She was a vision in a soft orange blouse and skirt beneath her lab coat.

"Here's Dr. Barsotti, Gina."

The girl looked frightened. "Are you going to give me a shot?"

He shook his head. "No. I just came in to see how you are doing."

"Her mamma will be right back," her visitor said with an entrancing smile.

Nico nodded before checking his patient's vital signs. "In the morning you'll be able to go home."

"You see?" the princess assured her, patting her other arm.

"Am I going to die?"

"Of course not," Nico answered her. "I believe this condition is going to go away by your midteens. Don't be frightened by things some kids say to you. They don't know what *I* know."

A small smile broke out on her cute face. "Fausta brought me this white Lagotto hunting dog." Fausta again. "She says her father has one." That didn't surprise Nico. The king was known to hunt. "I love him."

The princess's compassion and generosity impressed him. "I'd like to be a patient so she'd bring me one just like yours, Gina."

"I might be able to arrange something," their royal guest drawled without looking at him. She stood up as Gina's mother came back in the room. "I loved spending time with you, Gina. Do everything the doctor says and I know you'll get well too."

"Do you have to go?"

"There's another patient I have to visit, but I'll keep you in my prayers."

"Thank you for the dog."

"You're welcome."

"Bless you, Princess," her mother whispered. Their visitor was winning everyone over.

Like last evening, the princess slipped out of the room before Nico could stop her. He spent a few more minutes talking to his patient, then he left to find out where the princess had gone. The charge nurse said she was seeing a patient down the hall.

Nico waited and made phone calls for twenty minutes until she appeared and walked toward him. The second their eyes met, he realized how much he'd wanted to see her again.

He'd never been so drawn to another woman. That was the hell of it. She was a princess and had to be off-limits to a man who wasn't of royal birth. At least he assumed as much, knowing her sisters had married royalty, plus listening to the speculation in the media of a royal marriage in her future. But he didn't see an engagement ring on her finger.

"That was a generous gift you gave my patient."

"I brought one for all the children and was happy to do it, but you have to know that what you said to her relieved her fear. It's obvious you have a way with children."

"You have your own magic." He shifted his weight. "How much longer are you on duty?"

"I'm off now. *Buona sera*, Dr. Barsotti."

He watched her walk away on those long slender legs. Unable to help himself, he followed her. "Princess?"

She turned around. Her exquisite blue eyes lit up. "Yes?"

"I'm headed for the cafeteria for a bite to eat. Would you care to join me before you leave the hospital? Or is there someone waiting for you?" Might as well find out right now.

"There's no one. In fact, I'm headed to the cafeteria myself to get some work done. But first I need to get my laptop from my locker in the cloakroom off the cafeteria. If it's all right with you, I'll meet you there in five minutes."

"That sounds perfect."

Curious to know the nature of her work, he headed for the cafeteria. After going through the line, he found them a table. When she came in minus her lab coat, everyone stared at her. Whether she was a princess or not, her beauty drew attention, especially his.

She acted oblivious as she made her way

to the table and put her computer on another chair. "I'll be right back after I go through the line." Upon her return he noticed she'd chosen coffee and a sandwich too. The second she sat down, she started eating. "Forgive me. I'm starving."

"I can relate."

Her gaze met his. "This afternoon I dropped in to see Tommaso and bring him a stuffed dog like the one in the story, but he wasn't there. Obviously you released him this morning."

Nico nodded as he drank his coffee. "If you'll give it to me, I'll pass it on to him when he comes in the office for a checkup. That'll make his day."

"He made mine. Thank you for offering. I'll give it to you before you leave this evening. It's in my locker."

"I have a better idea. Why don't you bring it to the pediatric floor tomorrow and leave it at the nursing station? I'll meet you there after your shift has ended and take it with me. If you're free, we could eat here in the cafeteria again."

Her lips curved into another of those smiles he felt reach inside him. "I don't normally have plans after work and would enjoy that very much."

She radiated a warmth that crept under his skin, causing his pulse to race. How could it be that she wanted to be with him when she could have any man she desired?

"Bene." He needed to focus before he got lost in those blue orbs. "Are you liking your volunteer assignment?"

She lit up. "I love it. If I'm blessed enough to be a mother one day, I plan to have a lot of children."

Nico found himself envying the prince who would turn out to be her fortunate husband and father those babies. "What kind of work do you do that requires your laptop after volunteering here half the day?"

"I help fund-raise for my younger sister, Lanza. She's in charge of setting up low income housing for veterans and others and setting up soup kitchens for the homeless. I spend my mornings calling on potential donors like CEOs who believe in helping with a financial contribution. In the evening I send them information and set up more appointments. That's what I'm going to do right now."

Nico finished the last of his sandwich. "I

can't think of a worthier cause." He actually couldn't and found her remarkable for caring so much. The male CEOs she met probably fell madly in love with her and would grant her what she asked for without thinking about it.

If he weren't paying off a debt while he hired people to search for his parents, he would make a donation. "I suspect you're anxious to get busy, so I'll leave you to your work and see you tomorrow at the end of the day."

"I'll look forward to it, *dottore*."

He hoped she meant that because the last thing he wanted to do was put distance between them. "*Buona sera*, Princess."

Thursday evening Fausta's pulse was racing as she left her last patient and walked down the corridor toward the nursing station. But the doctor wasn't there waiting for her and her heart plummeted to her feet. She couldn't believe how disappointed she was as she approached the charge nurse. How could she care about him this fast? What was wrong with her?

"Do you still have the stuffed dog I left here when I came on duty?"

"No. Dr. Barsotti took it and said he would meet you in the cafeteria."

After struggling to recover, she thanked the nurse and left for the cloakroom. Once she'd hung up her lab coat and pulled out the laptop from her locker, she was so eager to see him, she could hardly catch her breath.

A chuckle escaped her lips when she saw him seated in a stone colored summer suit at the same table as yesterday drinking coffee. What a gorgeous man! He'd propped the dog on its backside in the chair next to him, like he was a diner too. Her eyes met the deep blue of the doctor's and they both laughed. He had an imp inside him that played havoc with her emotions.

"You were amazing to find this terrier for Tommaso, Princess. He looks like the dog painted on the book cover."

"I think he does too." She left her computer on the other chair. "I'll be right back. What are they serving tonight?"

"I hear it's chicken and rice, but I think I should give it a miss." He took a deep breath. "If I asked if you'd consider having dinner with me elsewhere, what would you say?"

She cocked her head, causing that golden

mesh to swish against her shoulders. "*Are* you?"

"Am I what?"

"Asking me out to dinner?"

His adrenaline surged. "Yes." Why not. This would probably be the only chance in his whole life to spend an evening away from the hospital with this stunning princess. Naturally she would have to be free of any commitments in order to accept.

"I'd love it" came the response, which astonished him again. She really wasn't involved with someone? Earlier she'd told him there was no one, but he had to be sure.

"Are you honestly telling me there's no prince in your future?"

"Nico—it's true I'm under constant pressure to marry a prince on my parents' short list, especially now that both of my sisters are married." He knew it! "And of course, there's continual speculation about my marrying a prince in the media. There will always be gossip. But in all honesty, I swear to you there's no prince in my life and there *never* will be!" she said with such emotion, he knew she'd meant it.

Before he could say anything else, she blurted, "What about a woman in yours?

How come you're not going home to someone important this evening?"

"I date on occasion, but so far there's been no one special."

She smiled. "I'm going to take you at your word. Thank you for being truthful with me. Now that we have that settled, where shall we go? I don't know about you, but I'm hungry."

"How about Babbo's?"

Her heart leaped. He'd just invited her on a date. "I'd love it."

"Then let's go."

As she reached for her laptop, he picked up the dog and they left the hospital.

Fausta couldn't believe he'd asked her out and was literally floating as they walked the short distance to the trattoria. For a while she could be the commoner she'd always wanted to be, going out to dinner with a fabulous man who wanted to be with her.

This was the normal life she'd always wanted! The way the women stared at him during their walk, she knew they'd give anything to be in her place.

When they reached Babbo's, Nico found them a booth and they both ordered lasagna. After they began eating, she asked, "How was your day?"

"Busy. A fifty-year-old male patient of mine had his gall bladder removed this morning. His surgeon didn't want to release him until tomorrow. Though he should do well, I need to know if there are any complications before I go home."

"Where would our world be without doctors like you? I know my father relies on his. We're all indebted to him."

Nico blinked. "What's wrong with him?"

"A bad heart. These days my brother-in-law Prince Stefano is helping him more and more with the load."

"I'm sorry he's not well."

She sighed. "I am too and shouldn't have said anything. No one outside the family knows."

"Don't worry. Your secret is safe with me."

Fausta finished her coffee. "I believe you." She'd lost her trust in men four years ago, but somehow she felt she could trust this doctor who took her breath away and had a bedside manner that instilled confidence in his patients.

One dark brow lifted. "Did you find any new benefactors this morning?"

She welcomed the change of subject. "Not

today. Maybe tomorrow. Fund-raising takes time, but I had such a wonderful afternoon with the children, I can't complain about anything."

"Nor I."

Suddenly his phone rang and he answered. When he hung up, he said, "I was afraid of this and need to check on my patient now. Tell me something. How do you get home at night?"

"Don't worry about me. I call for the limo. The driver will pick me up here."

"I'm sorry I have to go." He got to his feet and picked up the dog. "Do you work tomorrow?"

Her pulse picked up speed. "Yes. Tuesday through Friday."

"Unfortunately I have a two day seminar that will prevent me from meeting you. If you're free Sunday evening, I'd like to see you again."

"I want that too." Her swift response thrilled him. "When you come to the palace, drive around to the left entrance and I'll be there waiting for you. Just name the time."

"Six thirty?"

"That sounds perfect. Thank you for dinner this evening."

"I'm the one wanting to thank you for coming with me." After reaching for the dog, he glanced at her. "I don't want to leave, but work calls."

"Don't apologize. I bet your patient can't wait to see you walk in his room. I know that's how I would feel."

If she didn't miss her guess, she sensed he would rather stay with her. Heaven help her but she hated that the evening had to end so fast. Sunday sounded so far away.

"I'll see you soon, Princess. And I'll make certain Tommaso receives his gift when he comes in for his checkup."

"Grazie. A presto, dottore."

CHAPTER TWO

NICO LAY AWAKE half the night. He kept seeing the princess's incredible light blue eyes
staring into his, holding him spellbound.
The words that she wanted to be with him
too haunted him throughout the two days of
meetings. But his insecurity over not knowing who his parents were made him feel less
worthy of her interest. It was hard for him to
believe she wanted to be with him.

The women he dated on occasion didn't
come close to her kind of compassion or understanding, let alone her beauty. She was
unique in ways that made him hunger to
know her better. Much better.

On Sunday evening he drove to the fifteenth century palace and followed her
instructions that led him to the side entrance. She stood outside the doors next
to a guard waiting for him, dressed in a

wispy blouse and skirt in a heavenly shade of hyacinth.

Her flowery fragrance filled the interior of his car as he helped her inside. Within seconds he drove his car out of the parking area and the estate onto the street.

"Fasten your seat belt, Princess."

"I will if you'll do me a favor and start calling me Fausta."

"You're sure?"

She let out a gentle laugh he loved hearing. "Since we're going to be seeing each other more often from now on at the hospital, it sounds too formal. Do you mind if I call you Nico?"

"Do you have to ask?" It didn't seem possible that they were on a first name basis. Excitement shouldn't have rippled through him.

"What do you ask the patients to call you? That is *if* they don't recognize you."

"Even if they do, I introduce myself as Fausta, as I did with Tommaso. My full name is Vittoria Eugenia Fausta Rossiano, but I prefer Fausta."

He filed that information away for future reference and turned onto another boulevard, but the traffic was heavy everywhere. "With your many responsibilities as a princess and fund-raiser, how do you have time to volunteer too?"

She turned to him. "Mamma has always said that charity never fails. By balancing my priorities raising funds for the homeless shelters Lanza is in charge of, I have time to volunteer. I envy my friend Mia for working at the hospital. When she mentioned a new volunteer program being started a few months ago, I jumped at the opportunity to indulge myself if there was an opening."

"Indulge?" he asked, full of admiration for her willingness to serve.

"Yes. You don't know how much fun it is to listen to older people talk about their past or read stories to the children when they're too sick to do anything else but listen. Lanza has an adorable baby boy, Ridolfo. He's eight months now and I already read to him. As you know, she married Prince Stefano of the Kingdom of Umbriano. Luckily they live here.

"As for my eldest sister, Donetta, she's married to King Enrico of the country of Vallefiore and is expecting. I'm excited about another niece or nephew coming along."

He smiled. "I remember reading in the news about their marriages."

She nodded. "Maybe they'll have a cute little girl or a boy like Ridolfo or Tommaso."

"You made his day. I listened while you finished reading to him."

"I'm the one who loved it. He asked a lot of questions about Pompeii, especially when I told him I'd been there and described some of the things I'd seen. He said he wanted to go there. He's a bright boy."

"I agree. In the beginning, did he recognize you as Princess Fausta?"

"If he did, he never let on. Children are wonderful. They don't set up boundaries."

Like you have, Barsotti. The fact that he'd even asked the question revealed his amazement that she continued to want to be with him. "I think most every adult has that problem who meets a royal like you."

"It shouldn't be that way. From the first time I realized I was born a royal, I fought against it and wanted to be a commoner. Though I can't change my heritage, I live my life like an ordinary person as much as possible."

That revelation came as a surprise to him. "Why do you feel that way?"

"You don't know how difficult it is to grow up not having your father around when you need to talk to him. It's not natural to have to make appointments to see him. If you want to know the truth, I wouldn't wish my royal life on anyone."

"I had no idea." She sounded so completely serious, he had to believe her. Yet it still didn't change his wonderment that she wanted to be with him.

"I guess you've already noticed I'm always ready for a meal."

He grinned. "By the lovely look of you, no one would guess. I'm starving too. What do you like?"

"Anything. Surprise me. I'd like to see where the renowned Dr. Nico Barsotti goes for a meal after an exhausting day." *Renowned?* "I'm always looking for a good spot to eat."

"That doesn't sound like you spend much time at the palace."

He felt her eyes on him as he headed for the old part of the city with its narrow cobblestoned streets. "How many hours a day do you stay in the place where you live?"

Nico knew where this conversation was going. Once again he'd left himself wide open with a statement that showed how off the mark he was over the life of a royal. "I sleep there. That's about it."

"You've just described my life."

Except that her world was full of activity he knew nothing about and wished he didn't want to know. There was no way he could ever have a romantic relationship with her. Though she insisted there was no one and she was free to be with him, he believed her parents would eventually prevail on her to marry some important prince. Again, he reminded himself that her sisters had married royalty. Why would it be different for her?

"There's a small restaurant around the next corner that serves one of my favorite dishes. Have you ever eaten *maialino allo spiedo*?"

Her eyes sparkled like blue diamonds. "Roast pig? I'm sure I have."

"But this recipe is different and you're in for a real treat."

After a minute he found a parking space along the ancient street, but it turned out to be a tight squeeze between cars smaller than his. He slid from the car and hurried around to help her.

Soon people were staring at her, but she

seemed oblivious. He noticed that men couldn't take their eyes off her. No doubt they wished they were in Nico's shoes as he ushered her inside Prospero's, a small dimly lit *cantina* over two hundred years old.

The owner saw Nico and hurried toward him with a wide smile. He couldn't take his gaze off Fausta. "*Dottore*—are my eyes deceiving me?" he whispered.

Nico chuckled. "No, *amico mio*. Prospero Gallo? May I introduce Princess Fausta Rossiano?"

"I *knew* it! *Benvenuto*, Your Highness!" He beamed. "I've never been so honored."

"Just call me Fausta, Signor Gallo, and I'm the one who feels privileged. Nico tells me you make the best roast pig in Domodossola."

Nico could tell by the way the owner seemed at a sudden loss for words that her compliment had thrilled Prospero. But after a moment he recovered and led them past several other diners to the best table of the house in the corner, where they were seated.

"We don't need a menu, Prospero. Just some white wine and your wife's *rigotoni alla carbanara* to go with the *maialino allo spiedo* followed by coffee."

"Al vostro servizio, Nico." His gaze switched to Fausta. "Princess," he murmured before hurrying to the kitchen, unable to call her by her first name.

By now the staff had to be aware of their illustrious visitor. Nico knew that a visit from a member of the royal family had made Prospero's night. Being with her had made Nico's night and he intended to enjoy it to the fullest.

"The owner is charming. Has he been a patient of yours?"

"No. We met in an entirely different way. When I moved to Domodossola eighteen months ago and joined the hospital staff, I asked around to find out what restaurants served roast pig. I tried several places, but they were a disappointment. Then I came to Prospero's and now I never go anywhere else when I'm in the mood for it."

"Why is that dish so special to you?" She'd just sipped the wine one of the waiters had brought to their table. Her lips glistened from the liquid, causing him to think thoughts he shouldn't be having, like how she would taste right now if he were to kiss her. His instant attraction to her was growing in leaps.

He drank some of his. "They use an old recipe that reminds me of the years I lived in Biella."

Her eyes searched his. "You mean Biella, Italy?"

"Have you been there?"

"Once years ago, with my mother and sisters. Mamma loved it because it was hilly with old *castellos* she'd visited as a child. As I recall, we had lunch there with a friend of my father's cousin. I remember walking up the steep, narrow streets to the citadel."

"I did it many times myself."

"So you're Italian! You must be here on a visa. Now that you're a doctor here, do you think in time you might apply for Domodossolan citizenship? Quite a few people from other countries hold dual citizenship."

"That's true—"

But before he could answer her question, Prospero brought their food to the table. He nodded to Nico then said, "*Buon appetito*, Princess."

"*Grazie*, signor. It looks delicious. So does the *rigotoni alla carbanara*."

Nico eyed her after Prospero walked away. "He cooks the meat. His wife makes the pasta with *guaciale*."

She looked surprised. "Doesn't that mean 'cheeks'?"

He chuckled. "In this case pig's cheeks. Normally the pasta is made with pancetta, but the meat is too crisp. *Guaciale* melts in your mouth." All the time they talked, he couldn't stop admiring the mold of her face and the way her eyes danced. There wasn't another woman like her in existence and he didn't want this evening to end.

The waiter brought coffee as they started eating. After a few minutes she leaned toward Nico. "This food is divine. How do you know all this? Were you a five-star chef before you became a doctor?"

"Not exactly. From the age of twelve to eighteen I was a pig farmer on an estate on the outskirts of Biella before and after school."

"You're kidding!" she cried with excitement. "You got to play with all the little piglets?"

Her comment tickled him. "You like pigs?"

She smiled. "Yes! Sometimes my sisters and I would visit a pig farm on the palatial estate and I always wanted to take one home and turn it into a pet like my rabbit.

My parents forbade it, but— Oh, they're so adorable!"

So was she. Already Nico realized he was falling hard for her. "For the most part they're well behaved as long as you don't separate them from the sow. There were times when I had to help a runt so it would thrive, and the vet would come. They have to be given antibiotics to prevent infection, and you have to put iodine on their navels. But sometimes the runts died. That was the hard part."

"How sad that must have been for you. When the wild rabbit I found and nursed back to health eventually died, it took me a long time to get over it. I'm surprised you didn't become a vet."

Nico finished his wine. "There was another experience earlier in my life that influenced me to go into a different kind of medicine, but I'll never regret my time on that farm."

"I think you were lucky."

"For many reasons I agree." *Right now I'm the luckiest man on the planet.* "The family I lived with were good to me and cooked roast pig at least twice a week. We ate well, which was a blessing because I was always hungry. Whenever I get homesick for those days, I come here to eat."

"I can see why. Do you ever go back to Biella?"

He was flattered and humbled by her interest in his life, as if she really wanted to know. "About every two months since I moved here. I enjoy the trip and visit friends, some of whom need medical help."

"How fortunate for them to have you looking after them." After she'd finished her meal, she swallowed the rest of her wine. "Where is *your* family?"

The inevitable question, reminding him of the separation between them. For a little while he'd forgotten. After sitting back, he studied her through narrowed lids. "I've been wanting to know the answer to that question since my first remembrance of life."

She studied him. "I don't understand."

"Someone like you whose royal pedigree goes back thousands of years would have a hard time relating."

"Please can't you forget my background and just talk to me like I'm a normal woman?" she persisted. Her endearing sincerity got to him.

Nico slowly drank his hot coffee. "I'm

here on a temporary visa that has to be re-newed on a regular basis. I have no idea of my true nationality, which is why I couldn't answer your question about citizenship."

A slight frown marred her brow. "But your parents—"

He lowered his cup. "I think around five years of age I must have asked someone where my mamma was because there was a painting of the bambino Gesu with his mamma in the big room.

"Apparently I understood some Italian and remember a lady in black patting my head. 'Only God knows, *figlio mio.* While you are here, we shall call you Nico.' Later I learned I'd been placed there with the nuns at the age of two, but I have no memory of it. The or-phanage is in a village near Biella."

A look of compassion and other emotions less definable pooled in the celestial blue eyes of the princess.

"Now I've told you more than I've told anyone else in years. You have that rare quality of being a good listener. I'm not sur-prised you were hired as a volunteer. The sick children won't mind being in the hos-pital with you there for comfort. Would you like dessert before we leave?"

"No, thank you," she whispered, clearly moved by what he'd told her.

Already he'd learned she had a sensitive nature that made her even more desirable to him. It set off warnings that he'd be a fool to get any more involved, even if she were amenable, but it was too late. She'd already walked right into his heart. But even if he dared to imagine a future with her, how could there be one? She was the daughter of a king and queen. No matter what she'd claimed, he was convinced her future would be settled by them when the time was right.

"Then I'll drive you back to the palace so your bodyguard seated near the entrance to the restaurant can go off duty and stop worrying that I'm going to whisk you away."

An orphan.

To think she'd been complaining about waiting for her father's attention growing up when Nico had been raised in an orphanage!

Already crazy about him, her heart went out to him. She wished the handsome, hard-muscled man who was so much more than a doctor would drive her to a place where they could be completely alone to talk some more.

Nico had stunned her by what he'd re-

vealed of his life so far, but she'd only
scratched the surface. After he'd taken her
into his confidence, there were endless questions she wanted to ask.

Instead he'd reverted to treating her like a
princess, which put distance between them
when it was the last thing she wanted. Tonight had been magical. Having to go home
was the part she hated.

After paying for their delicious meal, he
said goodbye to the owner and walked her to
his car, clinging to her hand. The small inti-
macy filled her with longing to get closer to
him. Soon they would reach the palace and
this glorious evening together would be over.
She couldn't bear it.

If she invited him in to her apartment so
they could talk further, would he turn her
down flat because he couldn't allow himself
to cross that line? She'd told him there was
no other man in her life.

As they entered the estate, she guessed
she'd find out because she didn't want to say
good-night. Already he'd become of vital
importance to her in every way. He followed
the road around the palace to the side entrance. Another minute and he pulled to a
stop. "Home safe and sound."

Fausta prayed he would want to stay in the car to talk with her for a little while, but no such luck. He got right out and walked around to her side to open the door. Their arms brushed as she alighted, sending darts of awareness through her body.

"Would you like to come inside, Nico?" Her heart was pounding so hard it had made her voice throb. *Please say yes.*

"Thank you, but I'm afraid I still have to return several calls after I get home."

Don't react, Fausta.

"I forgot about that. Thank you so much for the ride and a dinner I'll never forget."

"Neither will I, believe me. Before you go in, I wondered if you would like to go to a film with me Tuesday evening after work? We'll grab a bite on the way."

His question caught her off guard so completely, she almost fainted with happiness. "I can't wait and haven't been to a movie in ages."

"Neither have I. We'll leave after your shift. In case an emergency crops up, let's exchange cell phone numbers."

When that was accomplished, he said, "*Buona notte*, Fausta."

She smiled. "*Alla prossima*, Nico."

Fausta headed for the entrance where a palace guard opened the door for her. Without looking behind her, she went inside and dashed up the staircase to her apartment.

Her gambit to prolong their time together tonight had failed, but he wanted to see her again on Tuesday evening. When he'd first turned her down, she'd feared he'd decided she wasn't that interesting after all. But his next question had sent her spirits soaring. He *did* want to be with her, hopefully as much as she craved to spend time with him.

She found herself dancing around as she got ready for bed. When she came out of the bathroom, her cell phone was ringing. She reached for it and checked the caller ID. It could be any one of her friends who worked on fund-raisers with her. Seeing who it was, she clicked on. "Mia!"

"Wow! Do you ever sound happy."

"I am. Nico and I went to dinner tonight, and Tuesday night we're going to see a film."

"Wait. Tell me all that again. Go slowly."

She clutched the phone tighter. For the next few minutes she explained how things had happened at the hospital, their meal in the cafeteria and Babbo's, plus their subsequent dinner at Prospero's. Remembering that Nico had said he hadn't told anyone else about his past in years, she kept that information to herself.

"The dinner was over too soon, and he drove me home. I asked him if he'd like to come in, but he said he still had work. I was afraid I'd ruined things by pushing too hard, but then he asked me to go to a movie with him."

Mia chuckled. "What did I tell you? The guy's smitten."

So was Fausta. So smitten she knew she'd never get to sleep. "Tonight he found out how much I wanted to be with him, like I was a desperate woman."

"If anything he probably couldn't believe that you, Princess Fausta, would actually ask a nonroyal man to spend private time with you inside the palace. In most people's minds, it just isn't done because it's such a great privilege."

"I don't want to hear that. He's such an incredible man, Mia." Her voice shook.

With the background he'd come from, he was even more remarkable than anyone knew. "Being with him tonight has let me know I've lived a very sheltered, uninteresting life as a royal."

"Don't be ridiculous."

"I'm being honest. The woman who wins his heart will be the luckiest woman alive."

"Fausta—"

"Sorry, Mia. It's late. I'll see you on Monday. If you can make it, let's meet in the cafeteria on your lunch hour before we both go on duty and we'll talk."

"That sounds good. But do yourself a favor. Don't assume anything. To him you have to be the most fascinating female on earth."

"You think?"

"I know."

If only that were true. Tonight he'd revealed he didn't have a clue about his origins. But there was one thing she understood above all else. Whoever his parents were, he'd inherited qualities and genes that put him head and shoulders above other men. She adored him.

"Ciao, Mia."

"Ciao."

Fausta hung up. Tuesday evening couldn't come fast enough for her.

CHAPTER THREE

SINCE THE DINNER with Fausta on Sunday evening, Nico had been out of sorts. She had everything to do with his restlessness, but it wasn't something he wanted to talk about with anyone, not even Felipe.

The women he dated knew nothing concerning his background. When or if the right one came along, that would be different. However, Fausta had been such a good listener, she'd drawn him out.

Their conversation at Prospero's had caused him to open up about his life in a way he'd never done since moving to Domodossola. He decided it was because in the end, nothing could come of his association with her. That's why he'd felt comfortable telling her certain facts. Maybe he even enjoyed shocking her a little about his work on a pig farm, but she didn't act shocked.

In truth, he was the one who'd been stunned when she'd invited him in to her apartment at the palace. There was nothing he'd wanted more than to get closer to her. He knew she wouldn't have asked him inside if she hadn't wanted it too. But it wouldn't have been a good idea because he desired her in all the ways a man could want a woman.

It was one thing to enjoy a few meals at or near the hospital with her. But to take her to Prospero's before returning her to the palace had opened the floodgates for him. Now he'd invited her to a movie.

Little by little he was fanning the flames with a royal princess whose life had been mapped out from birth. Though she wished she were a commoner and insisted she would never marry a prince, Fausta had admitted that her parents were constantly pressuring her. Of course he believed her, but Nico didn't feel…worthy of her.

He was a child who'd grown up abandoned by his parents and had become a realist. Though Fausta might not be in a relationship right now, she'd just told him her parents had royal plans for her. All he could imagine would be an affair with her, which would be impossible to hush up, something he couldn't let happen.

There was another factor too. It wouldn't be fair to go on seeing her when he might not stay in Domodossola much longer. That all depended on finding his parents, and he was expecting some news of them soon. For that reason, he hadn't bought a home and settled down here.

The small Italian-speaking country of Domodossola was only two hours away from Biella on the northwestern Italian border. His parents could have lived within that radius before he was taken to the orphanage. But so far a thorough investigation here in this country as well as the region around Biella hadn't turned up any information. At this point he'd been investigating elsewhere.

When or if he did find his parents, or discover his origins or where he belonged, and he discovered it was in another country, hopefully one or both his parents would want to get acquainted with him. It might be that he'd make a permanent move to be with them.

Then again, they might not want anything to do with him. Though he was taking a huge risk, he'd nursed the hope of a reunion for years. Certainly he wouldn't expect a woman he was involved with, especially the princess, to deal with a future as uncertain as his.

All this was on his mind as he and Fausta exited the theatre. She looked gorgeous in a summery print dress. "Let's get some gelato around the corner before I take you home."

Their bodies brushed as they made their way through the crowds. The warm, beautiful early summer night brought out his longing to find a private place and kiss her into oblivion. So far he hadn't touched her. He didn't dare, or he wouldn't want to stop.

They both chose strawberry gelato and made their way back to his car. On the drive to the palace his mind flew ahead to the next time they would be together. Right now, he couldn't imagine his life without seeing her every day. He decided it would be safer to continue to be with her in public places where they would be around other people.

Nico drew the car around to the side entrance before turning to her. "I enjoyed being with you tonight more than you know. Thanks for sitting through that action film. It wasn't as good as it was purported to be."

He took her empty gelato cup and put it in the bag.

"I agree, but I didn't care because I had a wonderful time. Since you probably have to go, will you wait long enough for me to run inside? I have something I want to give you."

She had something for him? He couldn't imagine. "Of course I'll wait."

"Be right back."

Within five minutes she'd returned carrying a white Lagotto hunting dog, the same kind she'd given Gina. After opening the passenger door, she placed it on its backside and put the seat belt around it.

She grinned. "You said you'd like one. His name is Giorgio. He works on a local pig farm. Now you won't be lonesome on your drive home because you'll both have a lot to talk about. *Buona notte*, Nico."

He burst into deep laughter as she shut the door and disappeared inside the palace. No one had a personality like Fausta's. Everything about her had enamored him to the point he wanted to take her home with him and throw away the key.

Barsotti? You're in huge trouble.

After he reached his apartment, he phoned her, hoping she'd pick up.

"Nico? Is Giorgio giving you problems already?" she teased.

He closed his eyes for a moment. "I'm calling because you ran inside the palace before I could thank you. Your gift has special meaning for me.

"When I first started working on the farm, people came who didn't know me and just called me Giorgio. I asked Angelo about it and he said it meant 'farmer.' Trust you to know that. Thank you again. See you tomorrow after your shift is over?"

"Absolutely."

When Wednesday evening rolled around, Nico didn't have a patient in the hospital, so he had no excuse to visit the pediatric ward. But that didn't stop him from racing over there after hours to find Fausta. The long overnight wait to see her again had been deadly.

She came walking down the hall ten minutes later and broke into a smile to see him by the nursing station. "*Ehi*—how's Giorgio?" Her hair shone like a pot of gold in the sunlight.

"We've become best friends. I've made him my guard dog while I'm at work."

"I'm glad you like him."

"I hope you realize I like the woman who gave him to me." He heard her breath catch. "Shall we head for the cafeteria for dinner?"

"I have a better idea. I brought a picnic for us and thought we could eat it on the grass behind the hospital."

She'd planned a picnic?

Today she was dressed in a yellow top and print skirt beneath her lab coat. He loved the way she looked. He loved everything about her. "I love the way you think."

"Give me a second. I put the bag in the fridge of the nurses' lounge."

He felt an adrenaline surge as she darted back down the hall for their meal. Fausta never ceased to captivate him. When she returned, she was carrying a plaid blanket along with a bag of food. No one had planned a surprise like this for him before.

He took the sack and they made their way through the halls and down the staircase to the door leading out back. It was another beautiful balmy evening. She found them a spot and spread out the blanket.

They sank down and emptied the sack. Soon they were both munching and drinking soda. "Where did this meal come from? It's fabulous."

"I asked one of the palace chefs to make me a picnic."

"No wonder I've never eaten such delicious sandwiches and salad before."

"Jeanne is a great cook and my friend. Sometimes I take her to lunch to give her a break."

"That sounds like you," he said in a thick-toned voice. "Unselfish and generous to a fault." He'd never known anyone so easy to be with. She never pouted or acted upset.

Fausta blushed. "Thank you for saying that, but it's not true."

"I have proof to the contrary before my very eyes." He continued to stare into those light blue pools until she looked away. "What's your agenda this week?"

"Tomorrow I have to go back to the palace by three o'clock to help entertain some foreign dignitaries for the evening. Papa insists on it."

Maybe it was a prince her father wanted her to meet, but Nico had to stop worrying about that or he'd go crazy.

"On Friday morning I have an appointment with the head of the Tocelli cell phone company. I've been pushing him for a commitment and believe he's going to help fund one wing of the new veterans' hospital."

"Bravo." Fausta's charisma could turn a man inside out.

"What about you?"

"No seminars for several months, *grazie a Dio*."

She laughed quietly. The urge to take her in his arms and kiss her had become a viable pain he couldn't endure much longer. So much for his plan to slow things down. Driven by his desire to be with her despite his reservations, he brought up an idea he'd promised himself he wouldn't do.

"Fausta? Before I have to go back in and check on a new hospitalized patient, I wanted to ask if you have plans for this coming Saturday."

She'd started to clean things up. "That depends," she said with an alluring smile that made his heart thud.

"I wondered if you'd like to drive to Biella with me. While I call on my patients, we'll visit the pig farm."

Her blue eyes danced. "There's nothing I'd like more than to see some cute little pigs!"

You've done it now, Barsotti. But he didn't care. Insane as it was, he needed to be alone with her away from their world. "It'll be a two-hour drive both ways. Can you be ready by nine? We'll stop to eat along the way."

"I'm always up early and will wait outside the entrance."

"Bene." He got to his feet and picked up the sack. She folded the blanket and they went back inside as far as the cloakroom. When she lifted her eyes to him, Nico could see a nerve throbbing in the base of her throat. "See you on Saturday."

After they said good-night, he conferred with his colleague over a patient, then drove to his apartment and phoned Enzo, who sounded ecstatic to hear from him.

Knowing that he would be with her all day Saturday was the only thing that helped him get through the rest of his week.

After letting the older man know he'd be driving to Biella and would be bringing someone with him this time, Nico got ready for bed, almost feverish in anticipation of being with Fausta.

When he drove up to the side of the palace on Saturday morning, there she was with molten gold hair, dressed in jeans and walking boots. She'd worn a long-sleeved kelly green pullover that revealed the feminine mold of her body. She carried a jacket over her arm and looked like she was ready for a day in the country. Every exquisite detail about her spoke to him.

Nico jumped out of the car and walked around to open the passenger door for her with the palace guard looking on. "*Buon giorno*, Fausta." He put her jacket on the back seat before getting in behind the wheel.

"I'm so glad you asked me to come with you today. I'm thrilled to be getting out of the city."

"After the antiseptic halls of the hospital, I am too."

They took off and headed for the highway taking them out of the city. He was aware of security following them, but he didn't care. This morning she smelled like wildflowers in a meadow. Nico had never been with a woman like her. Moreover, he'd never done anything this exciting. She'd wanted to come with him. Nothing else mattered.

All the way to the border and beyond, the trees were in blossom with pink and white petals. She let out a sigh. "It's a beautiful June day already. Only a few white clouds are hanging in the sky. Everything is green and lush. I can't tell you how happy I am to be out in nature like this."

Her words painted a picture. "You took the words out of my mouth." They traveled past manicured farms that displayed a picture-book quality. "Does your family know you're with me?"

"I'm sure they do."

By now they probably knew all about him and didn't approve. Nico didn't want to think about it, but it was hard to look past the demands of her royal background. "I don't know about you, but I'm hungry. Let's stop in the next village and get some food we can eat in the car."

"I was hoping you'd suggest it."

They came to a hamlet and found delectable rabbit quiche with rosemary, black raspberry fruit tarts and sodas at a little local deli.

"This food is divine." En route she ate and drank with the same relish he did. "I know we're traveling to Biella. You said the orphanage wasn't that far from there. Could we see it too?"

He sucked in his breath. "You want to go to Mottalciata? The population is only about fifteen hundred people."

"You really did grow up in a small village, but it's part of your childhood. I'd love to at least drive by it."

"If you want, then we'll go there first."

Before long they reached the village in question. "This place, plus the Barsotti farm on the outskirts of Biella, made up my only world until I went to the university in Turin, Italy."

She looped some of that diaphanous hair behind her ear. "I haven't been to Turin in years. By now it's probably grown to a million people."

"Most likely."

"To go to the university there must have been a revelation to you."

He nodded. "When I wasn't studying, I walked and walked, marveling at everything."

Her eyes played over him. "I can just imagine the wonders that filled your young man's vision of everything."

They smiled at each other in understanding.

"Where's the orphanage?"

"It's in part of the old Romanesque church. We're coming to it now."

"Would it be hard for you to go in? I'd love to see where you grew up."

"Not hard, but I don't imagine things will be the same. I haven't been inside it since I left to attend the university."

Her gaze implored him. "It'll be fascinating to find out."

She was right about that. "Just coming here again, seeing the village through my outsider eyes at this point, brings back haunting memories."

Alarm filled Fausta's expression. "If it hurts too much, we should turn around."

He heard what she was saying, but they'd arrived. Nico pulled up in front of the church and shut off the engine.

"I'm not in pain, Fausta. At that time in my life, I grew up bewildered. So many children with no mothers or fathers. I was full of questions. Where were all our families? Where was *mine*? How did I end up here of all places? Didn't my parents want me?"

Her light blue eyes misted over. "We don't have to go in."

"I want to. After telling you about my past the other night, I feel a need to revisit this place now that we're here."

After a pause, she asked, "Would you rather go in alone?"

His dark eyes impaled her. "I wouldn't have come to Mottalciata without you."

The intensity of Nico's words penetrated to her insides, causing Fausta to tremble. She got out of the car before he opened her door. Together they entered the church vestibule and followed the sign to the orphanage entrance.

Nico knew exactly where to go. An elderly nun in black seated at a desk greeted them as they walked through the door to the office.

"*Buon giorno*, signor. How can I help you?"

"My name is Nico Barsotti. This is my friend Signorina Rossiano."

It pleased Fausta that he didn't refer to her as a princess. The nun didn't appear to recognize her and that was fine with Fausta.

"From the age of two to twelve I spent my life here. A year ago, I learned from a friend that the holy mother who looked after me passed away. I'm sorry that I found out too late since I wanted to thank her for everything. The sisters were very good to me."

She smiled at him. "I'm sure she knows, signor."

For Nico's sake Fausta hoped so.

"Would it be possible to go into the common room for a moment, or should we come back?"

"You may go in now. The children are at lunch."

"Grazie."

Fausta followed him through some double doors into the large room he'd told her about. A big beautiful painting of the Madonna and child took up part of one wall. Next to another wall stood an upright piano. There were shelves with well-worn toys and books. Seeing this place gave her the idea to send the orphanage some donations, but they would have to come from her own personal money.

He reached for her arm and they gravitated toward the painting. Nico studied it for a long moment. Fausta knew he'd gone back in time. "How remarkable. Nothing here has changed after all."

This was where he'd spent his early childhood. Pain stole through her for his heartache. "I'm thinking about the children in the other part of the orphanage, Nico. I'll pray they grow up to be happy and become as successful as you are."

He squeezed her arm before letting it go.

By tacit agreement they walked through to the office. Nico approached the nun still seated at the desk.

"Thank you for letting us visit. We'll be leaving now."

"Come anytime. You'll always be welcome."

Fausta left with him. They walked out of the church in silence. She feared this visit would trouble him for a long time. But when they got in the car, he turned to her, his dark blue eyes alive.

"There was an old doctor who came from Biella once in a while when one of us was sick. He seemed like a magician to me and could fix anything. Every time he showed up, I followed him around and asked questions. I thought how wonderful if I could do something like that one day."

Realizing that Nico had been thinking about the doctor who'd set him on his course, she could hardly swallow for the boulder in her throat. "So, *he's* the reason you became a physician. Do you think he's still alive?"

"I wish he were so I could thank him, but no. He too died after I left the orphanage." Nico started the engine. "Are you ready to visit some pigs? I come here every couple of months. The Barsotti farm is about two miles from the main square here."

"I've been thinking about playing with them ever since you mentioned it at the hospital."

His good spirits were contagious. Nico would never know what it meant to her to be let into his life, allowing her to see beneath the surface. He drove on while she drank in the bucolic landscape.

When they came to the Barsotti farm, Nico pointed out the farmhouse and the many outbuildings. The large property looked well kept. Several long buildings housed the pigs.

Nico pulled up to the office. "I'll run inside and see if I can find Angelo. Be right back."

"Take all the time you need."

She got out to wait, loving seeing the place where he'd worked, loving being with him like this.

A few minutes later Nico reappeared with an older farmer who was dressed in overalls and wore a huge smile on his mustached face.

"Fausta? I'd like you to meet Angelo Barsotti, the man who transformed my life after taking me out of the orphanage. I owe him and his wife everything. Today she's visiting their daughter who just had a baby, so you won't be able to meet her."

"I'm sorry about that."

The farmer removed his cap. "Princess." His gaze swerved to Nico. "Looks like you've done right well for yourself."

"Nico has sung your praises, signor. I'm very happy to meet you. Last week we went out for roast pig. He told me about life with you and how kind you and your wife were to him."

"Nico was a good boy and a hard worker."

"He's an excellent doctor now, but it's obvious he hasn't forgotten those years with you. Would it be possible to see some of your piglets before we leave?"

The farmer grinned. "He said you wanted to play with them. One of our sows just had a litter. Come with me."

Delighted, she followed them to one of the long buildings containing the individual grilled stalls to house all the pigs.

Inside she saw several workers walking up and down the aisles. He led them to a section where the new mother was tending her litter. There were seven spotted piglets who stuck their noses toward them.

"Oh—look, Nico! Aren't they adorable?" She ran over to the fencing. "Can I hold one, Signor Barsotti?"

He laughed. "Go right ahead."

Fausta leaned over and picked one up from the straw. "You sweet little thing," she crooned as it made snorting sounds. Soon all the piglets were making noises, causing her to laugh. The men laughed too. Her gaze fused with Nico's. This was a moment of pure joy she'd never forget.

She walked around with it for a minute, but before the sow got too upset, Fausta lowered the piglet back to the straw. "If I could, I'd take all of you home with me."

They left the building and walked back to his office. "There's a restroom inside, where the two of you can freshen up, Princess."

"Thank you. I'll be right back."

She went inside first. It thrilled her to have met the man who'd given Nico a real home and family until he'd turned eighteen. Fausta thought him and his wife remarkable people.

To give them time alone, she went back to the car and reached for another soda while she waited. The two of them talked and laughed. She got another lump in her throat when she saw them pat each other's shoulder.

"You made a hit with Angelo," Nico said after he got back in the car and they drove away.

"He was so nice. I can understand why you love visiting him. How do you have his last name since you haven't referred to him as your adoptive father? Or did I miss something?"

"They wanted to adopt me even though they had four children. I told them I'd rather not belong to anyone because I wanted to find my birth parents. Deep down I didn't feel worthy of love when my own parents didn't want me. People just automatically thought I belonged to them and the name stuck."

Whoa. He didn't feel worthy? Fausta was only now beginning to understand how much being an orphan had impacted him. Not many children would have turned down the opportunity to be adopted yet go on repaying them for their kindness.

He glanced at her. "I wouldn't blame you if you think that was strange and ungrateful of me, but I assured them I'd work triple hard for them to earn my keep until I could leave at eighteen. I've been sending them money ever since I became a doctor."

"Not strange, Nico. Just amazing that even at the age of twelve, you were so fiercely independent. It's made you into the man you've become." His comments had raised more questions she wanted answers to, but now wasn't the time.

Nico eyed her. "From here we're going to visit a couple. I want you to meet Enzo and Pippa. They're expecting us and have done everything for me since I started working for Angelo. In truth Enzo has been my savior and mentor."

"Savior?"

"He owns the land where Angelo works the pig farm, but let me back up. Angelo came to the orphanage to find a boy he could train who would help on the farm. He chose me and was given special permission to let me live with his family on the farm and go to school with his children.

"I was chosen, but I had to be interviewed by the owner before I could be hired. It seemed that one of the owner's grandsons had died at the age of twelve. I guess I was a reminder of him and he developed an interest in me. He often dropped by the farm to talk to me and we became friends."

"That's very touching."

"In time he took me to his home for visits and saw to it that I got the best schooling. After I turned eighteen, he paid for me to attend college and medical school in Turin. He and his wife have always had a doctor to take care of them, but I made him a promise that I would also be their personal physician for life after I graduated."

Fausta was dumbfounded by what he'd just told her. It answered so many questions about how he'd gotten from A to B. "Where does he live?"

"In the foothills of Biella not far from here."

They'd reached the outskirts. "So, *they're* the people you take care of."

His dark eyes gleamed. "I visit them every couple of months and always look forward to it."

They drove through the town and up a winding road through the lush foothills to a picturesque estate. When an imposing *castello* appeared through the trees, Fausta drew in her breath.

"I've been here before!" she cried softly.

He'd pulled up in the courtyard and had turned off the engine before looking at her. "I know. You told me you'd been to Biella the night we went to dinner."

"But I mean *this* is the estate where my mother brought me and my sisters for a visit. I recognize the distinctive crenellated walls and the belfry."

Nico's eyes played over her. "You're sure? How old were you?"

"I was around ten. Donetta was thrilled because the owner had some beautiful horses and let us ride. Of course, I'm no champion like my sister. She has a room full of trophies."

"It's true Enzo *is* a great horse lover. Let's go inside."

But no sooner had Nico opened the passenger door for her than a man with white hair who was probably in his eighties wearing casual clothes came outside to greet them.

"Nicolo—" she heard the man call out before hugging him fiercely. She was struck by the love between the two of them.

As the old man turned to her, he let out a strange sound. "When you told me you were bringing someone with you, I didn't know you meant Princess Fausta Rossiano!"

"Am I missing something here?" Nico looked confused.

The older man moved toward her. "The last time I saw you and your sisters, you were just young girls. It must have been fifteen years ago." He smiled. "The older one rode like the wind."

Fausta smiled back. "I just told Nico I remember coming here. You're Duca Enzo Frascatti of Piedmont, the local magistrate of the area. You're the good friend of Prince Lorenzo, my father's cousin!"

Nico stared at her in wonder.

"Indeed I am. Lorenzo and I are the best of friends. He's the one who advised me to buy a new Sanfratellano stallion from the king's stables in Vallefiore. To think your sister is now the new king's wife! It's a small world, my dear."

"It certainly is. I'm thrilled to meet you again after all this time."

Enzo reached for her hand and kissed the back of it. "This is a joyous day. Come inside and we'll all catch up. My wife, Pippa, and I have lunch waiting for you. She's in a wheelchair and not doing that well, but she's always eager for the next visit from our Nicolo."

Fausta's gaze fused with Nico's. She could tell he was bursting with questions. So was she!

Nico grabbed his medical bag. Together they followed Enzo inside. He walked them through to the main dining room of the sumptuous *castello* Fausta remembered, where his wife sat in her wheelchair at the table. Nico led her around.

"Pippa? Do you remember Princess Fausta? She's the person I brought with me today."

The white-haired older woman studied Fausta out of eyes dimmed by the years. "You were a precious little girl who loved all the animals. My how you've grown up into a beautiful woman."

Fausta blushed. "Thank you, Duchessa. It's so kind of you to have us for lunch."

"Nonsense. Nico is like a son to us. Why don't you be seated so we can talk."

Nico held a chair for Fausta. After they sat down, the staff served them lunch.

The *duca* raised his wineglass. "This is a very happy day. I'd like to make a toast to our Nicolo and the princess. To your health and other things."

After they'd sipped their wine, Pippa eyed

Fausta. "When our grandson died, Nico came into our lives and brought us happiness. Did he tell you we wanted to adopt him?" Fausta's eyes met Nico's for a moment. Everyone loved him. "But he was so stubborn, he wouldn't hear of it."

Except that Fausta knew the real reason. Nico's origins had made him feel unworthy of love.

CHAPTER FOUR

THIS OUTING HADN'T turned out as Nico had expected. Fausta fit in seamlessly with Enzo and Pippa. They were all of the same world.

Except for having been born to an unknown man and woman who gave him life, Nico had been beholden to the nuns at the orphanage, the farmer and the *duca* for being allowed to thrive on this earth. Even though he was now a doctor and could earn his daily bread from here on out, Fausta's father was still pressuring her to marry a prince. It didn't matter to him that his daughter had been dating Nico.

For the rest of lunch he talked about his practice and answered their questions about how he and Fausta had met at the hospital. Afterward he gave Enzo and Pippa a physical before he and Fausta left to drive back to Domodossola. Her bodyguard's car followed at a distance.

She turned to him. "Are you able to tell me what happened to Pippa?"

"Last year she fell in the shower and broke her hip. The fall injured both knees and she's in a lot of pain."

Fausta decided she shouldn't ask about Enzo.

"What would they do without your help? You can tell they love you so much."

Nico flashed her a glance. "The feeling's mutual. Luckily their married children live close by and take them to Turin to see their regular doctor when it's necessary. I like to look after them because I love them."

"They're lovely people."

"I know they enjoyed your company and remember your visit years ago. Did you see the way Enzo beamed when he saw you?"

She nodded. "But Angelo was so kind too. Imagine him and his wife taking you to their hearts! It's a wonderful thing they did for you. Their generosity makes you believe in the goodness of the human spirit."

Nico smiled. "Angelo couldn't get over the way you, a princess, gathered that piglet in your arms like it was a baby."

"It *was* a baby." They both chuckled.

The extraordinary woman seated next to him blended in wherever he took her. Today had been a day out of time. Fausta was such great company, he could wish it would go on forever and he had to face the truth. He'd never been in love. But after meeting and being with Fausta for the last two weeks, he knew he'd fallen in love with her. It had happened so fast, he couldn't believe it.

Yet in acknowledging it to himself, it only made him more conflicted. They were relishing each other's company now, but even if she accepted him for who he was, her royal heritage hung between them like a barrier that could prevent them from moving forward.

Before she got out of the car, he needed to tell her what was on his mind. She needed to understand that the visit with Enzo had underlined a problem he could no longer ignore. He pulled in the parking area and shut off the engine. Two other cars were outside, but no one was around except the palace guard.

Her eyes darted to him. "You've been quiet for the last little while. I can tell something's on your mind. I would invite you in so we could talk. But since I know you'll turn me down like you did before, I won't."

He eyed her in frustration. "Fausta—"

"I saw the look on your face when you realized my father's cousin had a connection with Enzo. I know what you're going to say," she interrupted him. "Before long my father will learn through Lorenzo that you and I spent a whole day in the country together and visited Enzo."

His lips thinned. "That's right. Say what you want, but I'm *not* a person on the king's short list of possible suitors for his daughter."

"No, you're not. But that's all nonsense to me. I've told you how I feel about living a normal life."

"Even so, you'll understand why I'm reluctant to go on spending more time with you when we know your parents couldn't be happy about it."

She bowed her head. "I understand more than you think. Thank you for a beautiful day I'll always remember. When we see each other at the hospital, we'll agree to nod and walk on." In the next breath she got out of the car faster than he could believe. "*Addio*, Nico."

As she walked toward the palace doors,

he jumped out of the car and hurried toward her. "Wait, Fausta!"

She wheeled around, her features taut. "Why are you prolonging this when you're afraid to be with me?"

"Afraid?" The breath caught in his lungs.

"Well, aren't you?" she asked.

He let out a sound of exasperation. "It's not fear! To continue pursuing you would be pointless for several reasons! But I didn't mean for what I said to come out the way it did. *Per l'amore di Dio,* will you come back to the car and let me explain?"

At first he didn't think he was getting through to her. He stood there in agony until he saw her expression change. "I will for a few minutes."

"Grazie," he whispered.

After opening the car door for her, he got back in his side and turned to her.

Fausta cocked her head. "What is it you want to say that I don't already know?"

"On the day I first met Enzo, Angelo came out to the pen where I was feeding the pigs. He said the owner of the property had come to interview everyone who worked on his land.

"I didn't know Angelo wasn't the owner.

He said Duca Frascatti was a great man whose family descended from a former Italian king and had riches I wouldn't be able to imagine. He'd hired Angelo from the village to come and run his pig farm for him. It was a great honor. As such, Angelo told me I had to honor the *duca* like he was a holy person."

"Did that frighten you?"

Nico frowned. "No, but it made me nervous. I didn't want to say anything wrong for fear I'd—"

"Commit a sin?" She smiled. "I saw the cross on the wall in Angelo's office. I imagine the nuns put the fear in you. You poor thing."

Fausta understood a lot. "When the *duca* came, he talked to everyone, but when he interviewed me, he started to weep. I thought I'd done something wrong until he told me I looked like his grandson who'd drowned."

"That's what Pippa said."

"What he said made me very sad. From then on, he asked if he could keep coming to see me and be friends with me. No one had ever taken a personal interest in me that way in my life. With Angelo it was different because I worked for him in a business-type arrangement. He wasn't looking for another son."

"But he wanted to adopt you."

"I know, and I'll never forget. Angelo was the best. As for Enzo, he was the one who talked to my teachers at the village school and took interest in everything I did. One day I was invited to the *castello*. When I look back now, I know Angelo didn't like it, but he had no choice except to let me go."

"I bet he gave you a talking-to before you left," Fausta surmised.

Nico nodded. "He told me it was a great privilege no one was given unless they were also born of a king. He said that I had to be the one exception, but I mustn't presume anything or expect such a gift to ever come my way again."

She stirred. "So *that's* when you learned that there was a line drawn between a commoner and a royal, one you could never hope to cross."

"Exactly. You can imagine how Angelo must have felt today when he came face-to-face with Princess Rossiano, who'd driven here with me. I know he's still trying to figure it out."

"He handled his shock very well. So did you when you found out I'd been to the *castello* before."

Nico nodded. "When I first saw the *castello* and entered it as young teen, I thought I'd died and gone to heaven. But instead of obeying Angelo's counsel, I waited for the attention Enzo showered on me and went there many times.

"Then came a day when he told me my grades at school were excellent, and he was sending me to the university in Turin. I couldn't wait to go. I was overwhelmed by his generosity to me."

"Angelo probably couldn't believe it," she murmured.

"I know he wasn't happy about it. I admit I was surprised he didn't want me to take advantage of the scholarship. He said I'd presumed too much and hadn't learned my lesson. When he warned me that I could never belong to the *duca*'s world, it pierced me with pain and guilt."

"Of course it did!"

"I knew he was jealous of the *duca* who could do things for me he couldn't. It really hurt him when Enzo talked with Prince Lorenzo, who arranged to find me a position at the hospital in Domodossola."

"*That's* why you ended up in my country? I had no idea. How wonderful for you."

"I'm indebted to Enzo in so many ways, you can't imagine. And even though I told Angelo I loved him and would always repay him for his kindness, I knew it was hard on him. But I saw the division between the two men in countless ways and knew what Angelo had said was true about that invisible line."

Fausta let out a deep sigh. "It *is* true, Nico. I found it out in my own painful way four years ago."

"What do you mean?"

"Forgive me if I accused you of being afraid. It's because of an experience in my life that changed the way I look at everything now."

"Go on," Nico urged. "I want to hear it all."

"Let me go back to the beginning. Tano, the chauffeur for my father, lives on the estate with his wife and children. His son Dego was my age. My first memories of childhood include them and my sisters. As we grew up, my friendship with Dego turned to love. We were excited to go to the university here in Domodossola together and eventually marry.

"One day my father told me he'd sent Dego to Rome, Italy, to attend the university there."

A groan escaped Nico because he knew what was coming.

"It turned out my father offered to the pay the college tuition and lodgings for Dego as a thank-you for their service to our family. With tears in Tano's eyes, he praised my father for what he'd done. But the man had no comprehension that he might as well have cut the heart out of my body."

"Fausta—" With every revelation she was removing the scales from Nico's eyes about her perfect life. It answered one question. She'd been in love with a commoner before. Deeply in love.

"I was desolate, knowing immediately what had happened. My father had arranged everything. My sisters had warned me Papa would find a way to separate me and Dego, but I didn't want to believe he could do anything so terrible. Within a year Dego had met and married a girl from Italy."

"I'm so sorry," Nico whispered.

She lifted her eyes to him. "It's all in the

past. When I got over the first wave of pain, I was furious with Dego because he didn't fight for me. In my naivete, I'd thought he'd loved me so much, he would have found a way for us to be together and get married no matter what my father did. I hated it that he'd been so afraid.

"In time I realized he couldn't have loved me the way I needed to be loved, otherwise he would have stayed in Domodossola and married me. My father wouldn't have prevented our marriage if Dego had insisted on it. At that point I stopped living in a fantasy world. It taught me a huge lesson."

Nico rubbed his forehead. "I hear everything you're saying," he commiserated, "but as you told me, your father hasn't stopped pressuring you to marry someone he has picked out for you. Palace security knows every move you make and keeps him informed where I'm concerned."

Her head reared, causing her molten hair to float against her shoulders. "He can pressure until doomsday, but I'll do what I want."

"I believe you, but if you defy him, he could cut you off in a way I'm not sure any princess would be prepared for."

"When that day comes, I'll deal with it.

Since I now have a greater understanding of how *you* feel, I won't put you in a position that will make you feel guiltier than you already do."

He grasped the hand closest to him. "You have no comprehension of how I feel," his voice grated. "Guilt has nothing to do with it. The reality is I don't want to make things more difficult for you."

She stared into his eyes. "Do you want to be with me, Nico?"

"You *know* I do."

"I feel the same way. Can't you tell?" Her voice throbbed.

"Yes." He caressed the side of her face. "If you don't have any plans for Monday evening, I'd like to take you to dinner. Your choice. I want to know what Princess Fausta does when she mixes with the commoners."

Her eyes lit up an electric blue. "You're on."

"I'll wait for you out in the parking lot after you go off duty."

"Perfect."

After she'd given his hand a long squeeze he felt through his whole body, she let go and got out of the car. He watched until she'd disappeared inside the palace. On the drive back to his apartment, he didn't know how he was going to wait until Monday evening when they'd be together again.

Realizing he needed a few groceries, he stopped at a local *mercato*. Once he reached home, he showered and got ready for bed before phoning the patients who'd called his service earlier.

With that accomplished, he sat down at the computer in his bedroom and checked any emails that had come in. He'd been paying investigators to find out how and why he'd ended up in an orphanage at the age of two. For the last year he and Enzo had covered northwestern Italy, parts of France, Switzerland and the country of Domodossola with no clues.

Frustrated that nothing had turned up yet, he'd hired other investigators to cover northeastern Italy, including pockets of Austria, Slovenia and the country of La Valazzura. If those searches didn't come up with something substantive, he would be forced to look farther south in Italy.

After going into the kitchen for a snack, he went in the living room, where he'd prerecorded a soccer game between his alma mater, Torino, and Florence at the Stadio

Olimpico Grande Torino. The team had quite a few losses. They were probably going to lose this one too. He didn't really care because he couldn't concentrate. His conversation with Fausta was all that filled his mind. She'd suffered trauma of her own.

Right before the end of the match, his phone rang. He picked up and said hello.

"Nico?"

That breathless voice couldn't belong to anyone else. His heart thudded too hard. "Fausta—are you all right?"

"I am now."

"Be honest with me. Is there something wrong?" Certainly the news that they'd been together all day had reached her father's ears.

"Yes. I had such a wonderful time today, I can't settle down, so I thought I'd bother you. What are you doing?"

"I just finished watching a boring soccer match and my old college team lost. Your call has saved me from severe depression. After our conversation in the car, if you had invited me in your apartment this evening, I wouldn't have said no."

"*Now* you tell me!"

Her answer was totally unexpected, filling a hungry place inside him that had never been fed until she'd come into his life.

Her quiet laugh enchanted him. "Do you mind if I pick your brains for a minute?"

She was a constant surprise to him. "Fire away."

"I haven't been able to get the visit to the orphanage off my mind. How many children does it house?"

He hadn't been expecting that question. "Anywhere from thirty to thirty-five."

"I want to make a donation that will be meaningful. I realize the place needs all kinds of supplies, which I plan to provide. But I'm also thinking about individual gifts that will thrill the children."

Touched beyond words by her generous nature, he sank down on the couch. Visiting the orphanage today had given him ideas too about lending his services to them every time he came to take care of Enzo and his wife.

But the possibility that the investigators might find his mother or father soon stopped him from making a commitment he might not be able to keep. If he tracked down his parents and one of them wanted a relationship, he would relocate if he had to.

"Fausta—it's enough that you want to do this, but your family does too much charity for you to incur such an expense for one facility."

"This will come from my own personal fund, so let me worry about that. Try to imagine what you think the children would want in today's world. What would mean the most to them?"

He took a deep breath. "I'll reflect on it and tell you on Monday when we have dinner. Have you decided where you want to eat?"

"Yes. It's down in the university district. I'm sure you'll love it if you haven't been there before. Now I'm going to get off the phone and give you room to breathe. See you Monday."

His hand tightened on the phone. "Fausta?"

"Si?"

The last thing he wanted to do was hang up. "Thanks for the phone call."

"You're a busy doctor. I promise I won't make a habit of bothering you. *Buona notte.*"

CHAPTER FIVE

THE DOMO GRILL featured a live band made up of university students while the clients danced.

The place was always crowded. Over the last few years Fausta and her friends had spent many an evening here. She knew the owner and most of the staff. They treated her like they did everyone else and made her feel totally comfortable.

"If it isn't the *deliziosa* Fausta! I see you've brought another lucky admirer with you. When is it going to be *my* turn?"

"*Buona sera*, Fabbio. We want your signature chicken Parmesan sandwiches with basil and melted provolone, and beer," she said to the fun-loving, cheeky waiter.

"Local or imported?"

"Local," Nico declared before she could speak for him. When the waiter moved away Nico said, "The guy meant it."

She laughed. "Maybe, but I happen to know he has a wife and baby at home. Fabbio is putting himself through college by working two jobs. I'll leave him a big tip."

His eyes played over her. "Want to dance?"

This was one time she couldn't wait to get in her partner's arms. She smiled. "I thought you'd never ask." Fausta had purposely chosen this *cantina* so they could get closer to each other.

They got up and walked over to the packed dance floor. Every woman in the place fastened her eyes on gorgeous Nico in his silky blue sport shirt and trousers. No man compared to him. He put his arms around her and pulled her close. She'd wanted this for so long. After Dego had left four years ago, she never expected to desire a man again.

Fausta inhaled the scent of the soap he'd used in the shower. They moved around other bodies as best they could to the soft rock music. This was heaven with her head against his shaven jaw, his hand splayed across her back as if she were precious to him.

She knew she'd fallen fathoms deep in love with Nico. The man was perfect to her and the fire for him was growing out of control. When he eventually danced them over to their booth, she didn't want to let him go, but she had no choice. They sat down and started to eat.

His penetrating eyes watched her. "The food and beer are excellent. I can't believe I haven't eaten here before now."

"If you'd attended college in Domodossola, this would have been one of your hangouts."

"No doubt."

She finished her sandwich. "Have you decided what kind of gifts I can have sent to the orphanage?"

"After holding you in my arms, I confess the mention of orphanage donations is the last thing on my mind."

Heat filled her cheeks. "I keep thinking about that place."

"All right—since the students attend public school, I think it would be wonderful to set them up with a few computers that can be used at playtime this summer. The nun we met at the orphanage was using one, but I'm sure that's the only one. It would mean a company will have to go out to install them."

"I had thoughts along those lines too, Nico, and plan to arrange for everything. If

I bought ten of them, that would allow three or so students on a computer. They could take turns. Time on the computer could be a real incentive to do well in school. What do you think?"

Her generous heart was a constant revelation. "I think I would have given anything to have one when I lived there."

"Good. Then that's what I intend to do. I'll also purchase ten special desks to house them and ten printers and paper so they can print off what they like. I'll arrange for several technicians Lanza and I have used setting up shelters to spend several days downloading the software and showing them how everything works."

"You don't need to do that too."

"I want to. Someone has to show them how. The little children will love to do play-time on them. There are coloring and painting programs for them. The older ones can do science experiments and study the planets."

His penetrating eyes bore into hers. "Your gifts will revolutionize the orphanage."

"Exposure is everything. Besides having fun, they need to be conversant with technology. It will help them get good jobs and go to college if that's what they want."

"You're an extraordinary woman, Fausta."

"Why do you say that?"

"It's evident you love children, but it reveals the measure of your character that you want to do something to better their lives."

"I don't hold a candle to you or your kindness, Doctor Barsotti."

He shook his dark head. "We're not talking about me."

"*I* am. When Angelo said that Enzo had made you an exception to all the rules, he knew what he was talking about. Whoever your parents were, they created a special child."

Nico scoffed.

"It's true!" she declared. "Angelo chose you from the other children in the orphanage to work for him. Enzo picked you out of all the other workers to befriend. It wasn't just your looks that reminded him of his grandson. Both men wanted to adopt you. You carry an aura that sets you apart."

His expression grew solemn. "What am I to say to all that?"

"Nothing. I'm as impressed by you as everyone who so far has had the privilege to be your friend, and I wanted you to know."

"If you've finished eating, why don't we

leave here and take a drive." He put some euros on the table. "It's a beautiful night."

Yes! Fausta couldn't wait to be alone with him. Dancing with Nico had only increased her hunger to get closer to him. "I'm ready."

They left the grill and walked to his car in the parking lot. He drove out to the street and headed for the foothills where there was an overlook with the city spread below them. Nico pulled to a stop and turned off the engine. She felt him turn to look at her.

"If I do what I want to do with you, I'm afraid I won't be able to stop."

She angled her head toward him. "If you *don't* do what I'm dying for, I won't be able to stand it."

In the next breath Nico reached for her and lowered his compelling mouth to hers. At the first contact she moaned with desire, needing him like she needed air to breathe. Her arms wound around his neck and she clung to him as they tried to feed their needs that were bursting out of control.

"I've wanted to do this since the first time we met," he admitted, kissing every feature of her face.

She pressed a hot kiss to his mouth. "I've

wanted this even before we met." Being with him like this was better than she'd imagined.

"What do you mean?"

"After I was hired, I saw you in the cafeteria several times before you even knew I existed. Mia told me who you were. From then on I hoped we'd meet."

"I remember seeing you too and couldn't get you out of my mind."

"When you came in Tommaso's room, I almost had a heart attack from excitement."

"You weren't the only one," he half growled the words and cupped her face, kissing her with increased passion. "You're the most beautiful thing to come into my life, Fausta. I'm afraid you're becoming far too important to me."

"*Nico*—don't you know that's how I feel too?"

Once again he swept her away, filling her with ecstasy. Then suddenly he lifted his mouth and turned his head. "Another car has pulled behind us. If I don't miss my guess, it's one of your bodyguards taking pictures."

Damn them, she cried inwardly.

"We're getting out of here." In one quick movement Nico let go of her and turned on the engine. Within seconds he took off so fast she heard the squeal of tires.

Fausta knew they were headed for the palace and didn't try to stop him. He wasn't used to being surveilled and she didn't blame him for being frustrated. When they drove around the palace to her private entrance, he turned off the engine and looked at her. In the semidarkness, his eyes blazed. "Are you free Friday evening?"

Her heart pounded with sickening force. "I'll make sure I am."

"Good. I'll pick you up at six and drive you to my apartment, where I plan to cook for you."

His home was the one place where she could be truly alone with him. Joy of joys. "I'll help."

"It'll be enough just to have you there with me. Now I think you should get out, so we don't provide any more entertainment."

She looked over her shoulder and saw the headlights. "Agreed."

He leaned over to give her another hungry kiss before she slid out of the car. All the way past the guard and up the stairs to her apartment she rejoiced that Nico had made the decision to fight for her. She'd known he'd been born exceptional and he was proving it!

Thursday proved to be a hectic day with overbooking that prevented Nico from walking over to the pediatric ward in time to see Fausta before she went off duty.

Upset because it meant he wouldn't be seeing her until Friday, he phoned her later. To his chagrin, he had to leave a message on her voice mail. He told her he was sorry he'd missed her today because of complications with his schedule. But he would wait for her outside the hospital after work and drive her to his apartment.

She returned his call later, apologizing for not being able to phone him until now. They chatted for a moment about Mia and Felipe, who were planning to get married. How lucky for Felipe that he could marry the woman of his dreams with no complications.

Unfortunately a permanent relationship with Fausta wasn't grounded in reality. He knew it deep in his soul and couldn't go on pretending something that wouldn't happen. When Friday night came, he knew what he had to do to stop what he'd started by pursuing her in the first place.

"See you tomorrow, Fausta. *Buona notte*."

"*Sogni d'oro*, Nico."

When he went to bed, his dreams weren't sweet. They were dark. In the middle of the night he woke up in a cold sweat, disturbed that he was putting Fausta in jeopardy with her family every time they were together.

She wanted a man who would fight for her, but at what price to her? If he were to ask Fausta to marry him, would she be able to handle making the ultimate sacrifice that could mean being cut off from her family? She said her father was a reasonable man, but so far she hadn't fully tested him.

Family was sacrosanct to Nico and had to be to her and her family. Nico didn't want her to have to give up everything in the royal sense in order to be with a man her parents could never approve of. He was tortured by the thought of not seeing Fausta in the future, but he didn't see how they could be together.

Underlying his torment was another more immediate concern. He would never stop trying to find his parents. Nico had to have come from somewhere and felt in his gut he was getting closer to discovering his origins.

In the end he made coffee and planned out some new strategies on the computer using maps until it was time to get ready to go to his office at the hospital. He'd leave the office early enough to hurry home and get dinner started before he picked her up.

"Mmm... Something smells delicious." Nico had just let Fausta inside his miniscule apartment in the university area of the city, the kind most students rented.

"It's my own version of manicotti casserole, one of the few easy dishes Angelo's wife showed me how to make while I lived with them. But the *panfocaccia* comes from the *paneterria* on the corner."

She chuckled. "Here I thought you'd spent all day cooking."

Now that they were alone, she was waiting for him to pull her into his arms. It was all she'd been able to think about. Instead he gave her a five second tour of his sparsely furnished one-bedroom place with its tiny living room and kitchen featuring a square table for two. He'd already set it and had made coffee.

After pulling out a chair for her to sit, he served up the food and brought their plates to the table. "I realize my apartment is probably smaller than the cloakroom off the hospital cafeteria. I hope you don't suffer from claustrophobia."

"Several friends of mine live in apartments this size. Everything's cozy."

He darted her a glance. "In my case it's colorless, but it serves my needs."

Nico's behavior puzzled her. He'd been distant since she'd run out to the car after he'd picked her up. Something had to be bothering him. He hadn't even tried to kiss her. Maybe a scheduling problem hadn't been the real reason for his not showing up on the pediatric ward Thursday evening. She started to feel anxious.

"It hasn't hindered your ability to make us a feast." She drank her coffee. "This *manicotti* is fabulous, Nico. I've had seconds of everything. But now I want to know what's on your mind. Since picking me up, you've been different. I don't believe it has anything to do with my being a princess, or that my bodyguard followed us here and you feel threatened."

He sat back in his chair with his coffee, eyeing her steadily. "You're right. The truth is, I haven't been completely honest with you."

Her heart thudded. "About what?"

"About my life."

She kneaded her hands beneath the table. "I don't understand." Fausta cocked her head, causing her hair to sway against her face. "What exactly are you saying?"

"The facts are that I've always considered my time here in Domodossola to be temporary."

Her expression sobered. "Why? You're an established physician."

"That may be true, but since I earned my first paycheck as a doctor, I've been actively looking for my parents."

She blinked. "Are you serious?"

"Yes. I'm praying to find one or both of them and make them a part of my life if it's possible."

"You mean all these years, despite everything, you've continually hungered for them?"

"That's the right word. When you and I first met, you asked me if I had applied for Domodossolan citizenship. I should have told you then that I planned to put down roots in the country where my parents had been born, where my mother gave birth to me. It's been my goal in life."

"I had no idea, but how hard life must have been for you to feel such an emptiness without them."

He nodded. "You can't imagine. Every day I go to my computer or answer a phone call in the hope that today will be the day I hear the news I've been wanting for years. I have so many questions.

"In what country will I find them? Who was my father? How did my parents meet? Were they the same nationality? Are they both still alive? Had they been married, or had they simply slept together? Had she been a single woman who'd been left abandoned?"

"Oh, Nico," she whispered, lowering her head.

"I've always come back to the notion that my mother could have been like other penniless girls in their teens who was forsaken and had to give up her baby. To my mind that seems the most plausible reason I ended up at an orphanage. If that's the case, I want to find her and help take care of her if she's still struggling and wants to be reunited."

Fausta's eyes had grown misty. "My heart

aches for you, Nico. How did you know where to start?"

"I've only been able to work with two available clues. The first was that the Mother Superior told me I'd come to the orphanage at the age of two understanding a few words in Italian. That meant I'd been raised by at least one parent who spoke Italian."

"Of course. What was the second?"

"She told me the exact date I was put in the orphanage. I arrived with five other toddlers at the same time. Why an influx of six children at the same time on the same day, with all of us were wearing the same nondescript clothing?"

"That's all you've had to go on?" she asked.

"It's worse than looking for a needle in a haystack and takes a lot of money to pay the investigators to do the research. That's the reason I live here in a modest, low budget furnished apartment. I keep out enough money to pay for expenses and recompense Angelo. The rest is used to fund the inquiries that so far have turned up nothing, forcing me to go further afield."

"Where have you looked?"

"One of the reasons I decided to be a doctor here was because I thought it was a good place to start my search."

"You mean you might not have come to Domodossola if you hadn't been searching for them?"

"No."

She shook her head. "Then we would never have met."

"I can't imagine it either," he admitted and grasped her hand. "But since your small Italian-speaking country of Domodossola on the northwestern Italian border is only two hours away from the orphanage on the outskirts of Biella, it sounded possible.

"My mother or parents could have lived within that radius before I was put in the orphanage. Unfortunately, a thorough investigation here in this country as well as the region around Biella and Turin hasn't turned up information. At this point I've been investigating elsewhere. The chances are that I could have been born somewhere in northeastern Italy, or parts of Austria, or even in Slovenia or La Valazzura.

"But nothing promising has turned up yet. Right now I'm focusing on the fact that my parents could have come from any country where Italian is spoken. I've been whittling down the possibilities because I refuse to give up."

"You're a truly amazing man."

"Why? Because I want to know my parentage?"

"No, because you don't let anything get in your way."

He drank more coffee. "Angelo has told me he thinks I'm foolish to keep spending my time and money looking for them. The other day he told me that finding my parents wasn't meant to be, that I should accept the situation."

"But Angelo doesn't know your heart," she said with her incredible insight.

"You're right. I'll never give up searching. Enzo has continued to encourage me and has backed me financially in order to help."

"He's a remarkable man."

"I couldn't agree more. If I should find out that I was born in Domodossola and that one or both of my parents still live here, I'll keep my position at the hospital and live out the rest of my days here. But so far the fruitless searches have proven to me and Enzo that I came from some other part of Italy or Italian-speaking country."

"But you don't know that positively!"

"That's true. What I want you to understand is that once I stumble onto my history and family, whenever that might be, whoever they are, wherever they live outside Domodossola, I could be leaving here and my job for good to be near them. That's assuming they might want to be with me after all this time. In that case, it wouldn't be a good idea for us to go on seeing each other."

A gasp escaped her lips. "Why do you think that?" Her head flew back. The way he was staring at her out of those midnight blue eyes, she knew he meant every word he'd just said.

"Please don't look at me like that, Fausta. I can't promise where I'll be next week, a month, a year, five years, ten years from now. Every day my money goes to pay for researchers doing the footwork for me. I live my life a day at a time and wouldn't ask anyone to share it with me."

She leaned forward. "Why can't you continue making your life here so we can be together? Why is it imperative that you uproot yourself as soon as you learn about your beginnings?

"If you should catch up with your parents—if one of them or both want to be with you—

couldn't you visit them often, or help them to come here to be with you? You could do whatever it would take without turning your whole life upside down," she argued. "And mine…"

He didn't answer right away. Instead he let go of her hand and got to his feet. "Come on. Let's move to the living room, where we can talk and be more comfortable. I need to explain that I don't want to force you to live in limbo while I wait for that day."

Fausta left the kitchen first and sat down on the end of the couch. To her chagrin he sat on a chair opposite her and pulled it closer, clasping his hands between his knees. This evening he'd dressed in trousers and a dark blue polo shirt. She couldn't take her eyes off him.

"What else aren't you telling me, Nico?"

"I learned something about myself when I did my internship. Part of the year I did a rotation in psychiatry. I did that on purpose, not only to get a better perspective on my patients, but to find out what made me tick."

"I can understand that," Fausta murmured.

"Dr. Neri, the director of the psychiatric program for my unit, had long talks with me after hours about my particular situation. He said the uprooting of a child's first emotional attachment from within a family group can be catastrophic.

"According to him, the particular short-coming of institutional care like the orphan-age means that a child like me didn't get the continuity of care no matter how well-meant."

"I'm sure that's true." Her heart was pained for him.

"He said it's almost always impossible to maintain any kind of continuity because of the high ratio of children to staff. There's al-ways the speed and frequency of staff turn-over and the nature of shift work to consider."

She moaned. "You saw that borne out when the Mother Superior and the doctor at the orphanage both died."

Nico nodded. "As the director went on to explain, institutions like the church orphan-age have their own culture, which is often rigid and lacking in basic community and family socialization. A child like myself had difficulty forming relationships, even with the other children. I wanted the security I'd been torn from."

"Then why did you refuse to be adopted when it would have given you security?"

Their gazes fused. "Dr. Neri told me my early sense of loss had made it close to impossible for me to trust people. He felt I'd been traumatized to a greater degree than some of the other orphans. I couldn't respond normally to the hand that reached out to me.

"All I wanted was my parents. No one else would do. I grew up and slowly learned to care for Angelo and Enzo, but I never outgrew the need for my birth parents. My loss made me more cautious, even fearful of strangers, and caused me to avoid touching them or accepting affection.

"Though Angelo and Enzo became steady elements in time, he said I'd suffered too much damage early. Thus finding my parents and roots became the paramount driving force of my life. He said I was an unusual case."

She fought the tears stinging her eyelids. "What if you can't ever find them? What if—"

"They're dead?" he finished the question for her and stood up, putting his hands on his hips. "Dr. Neri warned me about that too."

"What did he say?"

"He suggested that I go in for psychiatric

counseling to accept that I might not find answers and enjoy the life ahead of me."

Fausta couldn't agree more. "Did you get help?"

"No. Once I started my next rotation as a general practitioner, I didn't have time. As soon as I graduated, I left for Domodossola to interview for my job at the hospital. I've been inundated with work ever since. But I'll be honest. I readily accepted the position at the hospital because I'd hoped to find my parents here in your country."

His eyes traveled over her. "Instead something else happened. What I never expected was to meet you, the daughter of the king and queen of Domodossola no less. Any more time spent with you puts you in double jeopardy."

Her chin lifted. "And if I were a commoner?"

"But you're not one, Fausta. Whatever happens, I'm on a journey that has to be taken alone. The day could come soon when I'll have to leave Domodossola on a moment's notice. Depending on the circumstances, I might never be back. For this reason, there's no way I can promise you where my life is going, and that's not fair to you when your life is here. You're a princess of the realm."

"If you only knew how I wish I weren't!"

"Listen to me, Fausta. Meeting you has been the most wonderful thing to happen to me in my life. But I've been filled with guilt that I haven't been totally honest with you about my unknown future. You deserve so much more."

"I don't deserve anything! All I want is to be with you. Can't you accept that?"

He rubbed his chest absently. "I want to be with you too, but I'm worried about us getting any more involved. If we stop seeing each other now, there's no harm done."

Suffocating with pain at this point, she shot to her feet. *No harm done? When I'm madly in love with you?* Fausta's heart cried.

Every word had driven the knife a little deeper. Ice had to flow through his veins for Nico to say something like that to her. She would never have thought it possible.

"Are you telling me you can walk away from your patients too? And what about Felipe's wedding? He thinks you're going to be his best man. I thought you'd made a commitment to Enzo and Pippa to take care of them."

His features hardened. "I plan to follow through with everything for as long as I'm still here."

While Fausta was capable of functioning, she opened her purse, unable to handle what he'd just told her. Pulling out her cell, she started to call her limo driver, but Nico took it from her and hung up. The touch of his hand sent waves of desire through her. He'd read her mind.

"I picked you up and I'm driving you home." His fierce tone stopped her from arguing.

"Then I'd like to leave now."

Fausta reached for her purse and walked out the apartment door first. In exquisite pain, she struggled not to break down as they headed for the parking area at the side of the building.

He helped her in the car. After shutting the door, he got behind the wheel and they took off for the palace at the north end of the city. "I should never have reached out to you. Nobody had to tell me I was playing with fire. I don't dare touch you again and you know why."

"You don't owe me any explanation. Once again, I've made a mistake over a man. I don't believe your reason for breaking up with me, Nico, but that's your affair. You and I have both been fools to spend time together."

The tension between them was palpable. So was the silence.

When they reached the palace, she brushed some hair out of her face. "Just so you know, I intend to carry out my idea to have computers installed at the orphanage. You won't have to do deal with any of it."

"Fausta—"

"Please don't say anything, Nico. I get it that you're on a quest for your life. Interestingly enough, so am I. More than ever in fact." She couldn't stay in Domodossola as long as Nico was still here.

The second he pulled up to the side entrance, she opened the door and got out. Before she shut it, she said, "I hope to heaven that one day your dream will come true. *Addio per sempre.*"

CHAPTER SIX

AFTER TELLING NICO goodbye forever, Fausta rushed past the guard and up the stairs to her apartment. No sooner had she entered her room than her cell phone rang. In her heart of hearts, she wanted it to be Nico. She pulled it out of her purse. To her surprise the caller ID said it was her sister Lanza.

She picked up. "Lanza?"

"I'm glad you answered."

"I just got home."

"I know. Stefano and I had taken Ridolfo to visit with the parents when security let them know you'd arrived. I'm afraid you're going to be getting a visit in a few minutes, and I'm sure you know why."

Fausta had told Lanza she was dating a doctor from the hospital, but she hadn't told her anything else. "I do."

By now Enzo would have told Lorenzo

about her visit to the *castello* with Nico. It had been only a matter of time before the news reached her father's ears. Fausta drew in a deep breath. She was ready for them.

"Thanks for the heads-up."

"If you want to talk later, call me."

"You know I will."

"Remember I'm on your side."

"Love you, Lanza. Give little Rufy a kiss for me." That was her nickname for him.

"I've already given him dozens when Stefano has given me a chance." She laughed.

After clicking off, Fausta changed into a nightgown and robe while she waited for her parents. Until they talked, she didn't have the luxury to break down sobbing. Not yet.

Before long Fausta heard a familiar knock and hurried to the door to let them in. She gave them both a hug. "Lanza told me you were on your way up. Come in."

They walked into her living room and sat down on the couch opposite her. Her father smiled. "We haven't seen a lot of you lately. When we learned you'd come home, we thought we'd drop in for a few minutes."

"I presume you've had a talk with your

cousin Lorenzo, so I can guess that's why you're here."

Her parents glanced at each other before her father said, "I must admit we've been surprised to learn you've been dating a Dr. Nico Barsotti from the hospital for some time."

Her mother sat forward. "We were even more surprised to learn that you drove to Biella with him and spent time with Enzo and Pippa. It would have been nice if we'd known about your association with this doctor before hearing about it from cousin Lorenzo. How did you meet him?"

Fausta sat on her legs in her favorite chair. "I've been doing a little part-time volunteer work at the hospital four days a week on the pediatric ward. He's a family practice doctor who was checking up on a patient and we became acquainted." That was the simplified version.

"I'd say it's more than an acquaintance at this point," her father asserted. "I understand you spent time at his apartment in town this evening."

"Yes. Nico made dinner for us."

A frown marred his features. "If the press finds out, the publicity won't be good for the doctor, whom Lorenzo tells me he helped get taken on at the hospital last year. As for you, any mention in the media could color your prospects for the kind of royal marriage we'd like to see for you."

Her cheeks grew hot. "Don't worry, Papa. You don't have to find a new position for Nico in Rome to keep us apart. He would never accept your money to get him settled in order to salvage his reputation or mine." Once he had a lead on his parents, Nico would leave the country on his own.

Her mother looked pained. "I can't believe you spoke to your father like that, Fausta Rossiano."

Neither could she, considering his heart condition. For the first time since she learned he had heart trouble, she'd forgotten because she was in so much pain over Nico. But never again!

"I'm sorry, Papa, and meant no disrespect. I hope this hasn't distressed you too much. The fact is, neither of you needs to be concerned. Earlier tonight Nico and I ended our relationship."

When he did come over to the pediatric ward to look in on a patient, he wouldn't find her there. She'd leave fifteen minutes early every evening to escape.

"Mia figlia—" Her father eyed her soulfully. "Why is it you continue to refuse the suitable men who've wanted to get to know you? All your mother and I want is your ultimate happiness. Prince Cesare is very anxious to spend time with you."

Fausta slowly got to her feet. "I know that, but I have to be attracted, Papa."

"Darling," her mother spoke up. "If you'll give some of them the opportunity to be with you, I know you'll meet one who will steal your heart."

If only her parents knew. Tonight her heart had already been ripped out of her body...

Right now, she was in such agony, she was desperate to be alone. "If you don't mind, I have a headache and need to get to bed." *I need to phone Aunt Ottavia and get away from here.* "Please forgive me."

Her father stood up first and gave her another hug. "Don't be upset with me, *dolcezza.*"

"I'm not, Papa. You need to know I never want to hurt you or Mamma." She kissed him and her mother before walking them to the door. "See you tomorrow. *Buona notte.*"

The second they left, Fausta ran to her bedroom and reached for her cell phone. Her whole body was shaking. Thankfully her aunt answered.

"Fausta, darling—how wonderful you're calling me!"

"I hope you'll still think it's wonderful when I ask if I can come tomorrow and stay with you for a few days."

"Nothing would make me happier! I can tell something's wrong, but I won't ask right now. You can tell me after you get here."

Tears had started to gush down her cheeks. "You're a lifesaver, Zia. I'll let you know my arrival time as soon I've made arrangements." She had to let the hospital know she wouldn't be able to volunteer her services for the next week. Something unavoidable had come up. "Love you."

"Love you, *cara*."

Fausta hung up and threw herself across the bed, utterly gutted by what Nico had told her. To never know his love because he felt he had to take his journey through life alone? It would surprise her if she were still alive by morning, let alone physically able to fly far away from the man who'd changed her world forever.

* * *

Late Monday afternoon a fragmented Nico had just dealt with his last patient when his cell phone rang. It wouldn't be Fausta. He'd made certain of that by the brutal way he'd broken off with her. Though ending their relationship had been the only fair thing to do, he'd been in agony since driving her back to the palace on Friday night. Another minute in his apartment and he would have taken her to bed.

Nico was aching for Fausta and didn't dare be around her now. Otherwise that whole speech he'd made that they couldn't be together anymore would have been for nothing. Aware she was his weakness, he'd promised himself that if he had a patient admitted to the hospital today, he would ask Dr. Silvio from the medical group to make the rounds.

He glanced at the caller ID and frowned. It was the *duca*. Something had to be wrong for him to phone this soon after the last visit to Biella.

"Enzo?" he blurted after clicking on.

"I'm glad you answered, *mio ragazzo*. Since I know you're busy, I'll make this fast. Can you come to the *castello* tomorrow? I wouldn't ask if it weren't of the most vital importance."

Nico's hand tightened on his cell in reaction. "Did Pippa fall again, or are you having trouble breathing? Tell me the truth."

"Calm yourself. It's nothing medical, but we *must* talk."

Maybe this call had to do with the fact that Enzo had been chatting with his friend Prince Lorenzo. By now the king knew about Nico and Fausta. Enzo could be warning him there was trouble ahead. That made the most sense, but after Friday night, Nico had already taken care of the problem and was one step ahead of him.

"Enzo—why don't you just tell me what's on your mind right now?"

"No, no. I have to see you in person." *Why?* Nico didn't understand. "Can you get someone to cover for you for the day?"

His brows lifted in reaction. Enzo was being surprisingly mysterious and insistent. "Yes, of course." After all the older man had done for him over the years, he could never turn him down. "I'll come first thing in the morning."

"*Grazie*, Nicolo."

The click sounded before Nico could even say goodbye.

Curious and intrigued by the nature of Enzo's unexpected call, he hurried out to the front desk.

"Dina? An emergency has arisen, and I'll have to be out of the office until Wednesday. Would you call the patients scheduled for tomorrow and make other appointments for them? If one of them needs to be seen immediately, ask Dr. Silvio's nurse to fit them in." The two doctors helped each other when necessary.

"I'll take care of it, *dottore*."

He nodded and left the building. After grabbing some dinner and doing errands, he drove to his apartment and checked any new emails before getting ready for bed. The urgency of Enzo's strange request had happened at a vulnerable moment for Nico, who needed to keep busy.

If that phone call hadn't come when it did, he might have found himself walking over to the pediatric ward. His pact with himself was so fragile, he knew every honorable intention would have been lost the moment he'd seen Fausta.

Eventually he went to bed, but sleep was

lost on him. He'd put Giorgio on his dresser, but the sight of him was so painful, he put him in the closet. At five in the morning he rolled out of bed to shower and shave before taking off for Biella. He brought his medical bag just in case.

During the trip, he relived that day with Fausta in the country. The unforgettable memories of her while they visited the orphanage and the pig farm made him groan with longing for her.

By seven thirty a.m. he arrived at the *castello* full of questions. A limo with smoked glass was parked in the courtyard. Something was going on. Nico expected that Enzo was out for his morning horseback ride. Curious, he walked around the rear to the stable first. Sure enough, he found his mentor emerging from the stalls with a trim, distinguished-looking, well-dressed man.

Silver threaded his dark hair and clipped beard. He was of average height and probably in his early sixties. Nico had never seen him before.

Enzo hurried toward him. "Nicolo—you're here even sooner than I'd expected!"

"After your phone call, I almost came last night."

While they hugged, he could feel the other man's steel gray eyes riveted on him as if in disbelief. It gave him an odd feeling.

After letting him go, Enzo turned to the other man. "What do you think, Signor Bruno?"

The visitor walked around them while he kept studying Nico. "The resemblance is uncanny, Signor Frascatti. There can be no mistake. Even without a DNA match, he's the one without question."

The man spoke Italian with a noticeable Slovenian accent. What did he mean "he's the one"? Nico's gaze darted back to Enzo for clarification.

"Dr. Nico Barsotti? May I introduce you to Signor Basil Bruno. He's the head of the secret service for the country of La Valazzura who has been our visitor at the castello."

What kind of business did Enzo have with this man? "How do you do." Nico shook hands with him. La Valazzura bordered Italy and Slovenia. That explained his accent.

"You have no idea how pleased I am to meet you at last, Dr. Barsotti. I'm here on official business for my country."

Nico shook his head. "What am I missing here?"

"I understand you've been searching for your parents since you were old enough to ask the Mother Superior of the Sant'Agate Orphanage where your mamma was."

Nico's heart started to thud. No one knew that information except Enzo, and more recently, Fausta.

"It pains me that over all these years, your heritage has had to remain a complete secret in order to save your life."

What? "Are you saying they're alive?" The mention of Nico's family filled him with an excitement he'd never known before.

"No. I'm sorry to have to tell you they are not." Just as quickly, Nico's spirits plummeted. "Your mother, Nedda Corelli, living on her own with you far from the capital in the village of Mesecino near the Slovenian border, died soon after you turned two years old."

The news shook Nico to his core. The woman who'd brought him into the world and had raised him for his first two years was gone? Just when her existence had been revealed? He couldn't bear it. In his dreams he'd imagined a reunion that would make up for the years he'd missed.

"And my father?" he asked in a hoarse voice.

"He died ten days ago in the capital city of Azzura after being bedridden with heart failure for the last six months."

Only ten days ago he'd been alive? Nico was aghast.

"With his death I've finally been able to bring you out of hiding."

What in heaven's name was the man saying? "Are you sure *I'm* the person you should be telling this to?"

"Without question, but let's begin at the beginning. Yesterday I flew here to meet with Duca Frascatti."

Sick with pain and shock, Nico looked at Enzo. "How long have you known about all this?"

"I knew nothing until last evening, Nicolo."

"The *duca* has been in the dark like everyone else," Signor Bruno explained. "But through my sources, I've known about his association with you for years. Last evening we spent hours talking about you and the remarkable life you've led so far."

Nico shook his head. "Forgive me if I'm still incredulous."

"Who wouldn't be? However, I've shown him all the documentation he needed and he can vouch for me."

A warm sun shone down on Nico, but he felt a chill. "I trust Enzo with my life, which means I'm willing to hear you out."

"I'm glad you said that because now that you've arrived, I have the great honor to fill in the missing facts about your origins and heritage. But for both your sake and the *duca*'s, maybe we should go inside and sit down to talk. This will take some time."

Nico didn't move a muscle. "Who am I, signor?"

The man smiled. "You're very direct and so much like your father, who was my close friend, it's uncanny." Maybe Nico was dreaming. "You were legally christened Massimo by your mother, a fitting name for you since it means 'the greatest.' You were her treasure and the joy of her life."

With those words Nico found it difficult to swallow.

"To fully answer your question, you are the illegitimate, only born, living child of

Carlo Umberto Fernando di Savoia, king of La Valazzura."

King Carlo had been Nico's father?

He staggered in place while the world reeled on its axis. Nico remembered hearing something about the king's recent death on the news. He thought he must be hallucinating.

Stupefied by what he'd just been told, he glanced at Enzo for verification.

A smile lit up his mentor's eyes that was unmistakable. "You're King Carlo's son, all right. From a photograph I've been shown, you look so much like he did in his twenties, I thought I was seeing double."

"It's true," Signor Bruno corroborated. "Here. You can keep this." He handed Nico a two-by-three-inch black-and-white photo from his breast pocket.

With a trembling hand, Nico reached for it. After one look at the man in the picture, he gasped aloud. Enzo had spoken the truth. Nico and King Carlo were father and son all right. Same height. Maybe not mirror images, but incredibly close in coloring and bone structure.

Nico cleared his throat. "Do you have a photo of my mother?"

"I do. This is yours too."

In the next instant Nico found himself gazing at a young, beautiful dark blonde woman in a skirt and sweater. Right away Nico saw certain resemblances to himself. He could well understand his father's attraction to her.

"You have some of her facial features. It's hard to tell in that picture, but her eyes were a light brown. However, yours are a piercing dark blue like your father's."

Incredibile! "Did my mother have royal blood?"

"No. She was a commoner."

Like me.

Nico still felt like one as he held the photos side by side. For twenty-eight years he'd longed for the sight of the two people who'd brought him into this world. His father had been a married man and a king who'd had an affair with a nonroyal. Nico had been the result. He was still trying to take it all in.

"Sadly, his Majesty died ten days ago. He has left his childless wife, Queen Liliane, on the throne. With her consent, I flew straight here to talk to you once the funeral was over."

So much news staggered Nico. He could

only stand there staring at him. Enzo's firm hand gripped his shoulder. "Come inside, Nicolo. You've had the shock of your life."

The three of them walked to the side entrance of the *castello* and went inside to the main floor *soggiorno.* Nico had no remembrance of how they got there. Pippa had joined them.

She wheeled herself over to the couch where he'd sat down. "We always knew there was something exceptional about you. Angelo told us the same thing after observing you at the orphanage. When I spoke with the Mother Superior, she predicted you'd been placed there by God for a unique reason. She claimed that one day all would be revealed."

Tears filled her eyes. "That day has finally come, and we couldn't be happier for you. You're the son of a great king. It all fits."

"Pippa—" He struggled to say her name, but he was too overwhelmed to think, let alone talk. After studying the photos once more, he put them in his shirt pocket.

"There's much to tell you," Signor Bruno broke in. "I understand you've never traveled to La Valazzura. The name of our beautiful country comes from its many blue lakes hidden in the mountains that are covered in pine trees. In the fifteenth century it was a free imperial enclave of self-ruling and autonomy, represented in the imperial diet, subordinate only to the Holy Roman emperor."

Unable to stay seated, Nico walked around for a minute while he attempted to process what he was hearing.

"Our country speaks Italian and some Slovenian. It has undergone a civil war started by your father's cousin almost thirty years ago. Giuseppe Umberto, now sixty-three, has tried many times to bring about a coup that would take your father down. He never succeeded, but there was an interminable amount of suffering that cost thousands of lives. There were many attempts on the life of your father.

"For a short time at the beginning of the rebellion, your father had a mistress, who conceived his child at a time when his marriage to the queen went through a bad period. They couldn't have children. Though she wanted to adopt, he wanted a child of his own body. Like you, he wanted his own blood. No one else's."

Nico's eyes closed tightly for a minute.

"The two of them became estranged because of it. For a short time he sought comfort elsewhere. When Carlo learned Nedda was pregnant, he had her installed in her own apartment in Mesecino on the other side of the country and provided for her needs.

"He didn't want to embarrass the queen, whom he loved despite their problems. Naturally he wanted to protect Nedda and you, the only son he would ever have.

"But when full war broke out, Carlo begged me to take both of you out of the country where you and your mother would be far from danger. Unfortunately, she was severely injured and died in the hospital before she could be rescued. I had her buried there, then I brought you to the orphanage here in Italy."

"Did my father know I was still alive?"

"No. I didn't dare tell him, or he would have insisted on my bringing you back to the palace. It wasn't safe at that time. The queen could never have handled it, and both of you, maybe all three, could have been assassinated by followers of Giuseppe."

The story was stranger than fiction, but it was Nico's story. By now he was riveted.

"There were many refugees. I decided to take five other orphaned children who'd lost their parents to safety with you. Since then, all five have been adopted. But apparently you didn't want to belong to anyone except your own parents."

"No," Enzo conceded. "As you've discovered, Nicolo was always his own person."

The other man chuckled. "Just like your father. You have to understand that the king was a target for years. His evil cousin wanted the power. Word got out that your father had a mistress and a baby. For that reason, no one could know where you'd been put in hiding for fear of assassination. Not even the church in Turin or the Mother Superior ever knew they were housing the son of King Carlo."

This was all too much. "What about the queen?"

"Incredibly the secret stayed intact from her. But now the prime minister of our government is calling for a new king. On one side, Giuseppe wants desperately to attain the throne and has been the root cause of the unrest. He's super ambitious and doesn't have the love of the country, but he commands his own army. The second your father's funeral was over, I took the queen aside and told her you were alive."

Nico groaned. "I'm the love child she

could never have. How she must despise me!" he bit out.

"Not despise. Like everyone else, Liliane believed you'd died with your mother. To learn that there's a part of him alive in you has come as a tremendous shock. Their inability to have children caused real trouble in their marriage. I'm sure her pain over his affair will continue to stay with her, but she believed in him and the monarchy.

"The fact is, your father was well loved and she knows it. No matter her bitterness, if you—his son—are equal to the task and have his same remarkable genes, she'll sense it after meeting you. If she thinks you could fill your father's shoes after the parliament guides and helps you learn how to rule, her opinion will weigh heavily with them because she's revered by most of the people too."

A strange sound escaped Nico's throat. "I'm sorry, but I don't know how she can she feel anything but the fiercest resentment of me. It wouldn't surprise me if she wished I were dead."

"That's for you to find out if you decide to meet her."

"*Cara Dio!* Did the queen know my mother?"

"She met her once."

"I can't imagine any good coming out of this."

"Would you rather I hadn't contacted the *duca*? Do you wish you didn't know anything?"

His jaw hardened. "I don't know if I have an answer to that question."

"Again, your frank honesty reminds me of your father. Will you do me the great honor of flying back to La Valazzura with me today, Your Highness? That's who you are to me even though you're still the uncrowned Prince. I've already arranged for your bodyguards."

Out of all the possibilities Nico had entertained when considering his origins, he could never have made up a scenario like this.

"The royal jet is waiting at the airport in Turin. Every moment we hesitate, your father's cousin is attempting to mount another coup that is gaining momentum. But the arrival of King Carlo's son could change the tide."

"How can the queen possibly be okay with this?"

The other man shook his head. "It's important for you to know Carlo mourned the loss of his precious little dark-haired Massimo every day of his life. He was there at your birth and took you to his heart. If your father were alive, he would beg you to carry on his legacy. With training and advisers to help you, you're the only man on earth who can."

Me? The illegitimate son? A doctor with no credentials to govern? A grieving queen who has been betrayed in the most cruel of ways?

A shudder racked Nico's body. How did all that work?

"Since the *duca* has told me how you've longed to know your parents, then now's the time for you to meet with the one person who knew your father far better than anyone besides me. If nothing comes from your visit and you wish to return to the life you've made, Liliane can at least answer the many questions you've had in your heart all these years."

Nico stopped pacing. Only four days ago he'd bared his soul to Fausta.

Whatever happens, I'm on a journey that has to be taken alone. The day could come soon when I'll have to leave Domodossola on a moment's notice. Depending on the circumstances, I might never be back.

The three day visit to Ottavia in Rome accomplished one thing Fausta had needed to put one foot in front of the other again. Her aunt encouraged her to follow through with her idea to give computers to the orphanage. Doing something of worth for those children would force her to set aside her heartache over Nico for a little while.

Fausta flew from Rome to Turin to meet with officials at church headquarters. They were delighted that Princess Rossiano from Domodossola wanted to donate such a gift to the Sant'Agate Orphanage and they talked with the Mother Superior to make the arrangements.

After receiving the necessary permission, Fausta flew home to Domodossola to touch base with her contacts. The next day she drove to Mottalciata and booked a room at one of the village's hotels. She knew she'd have to be there for quite a while.

The Mother Superior couldn't have been

more excited. Since there was so little room at the orphanage, she had the desks with the computers and printers set up in the large common room. Five were placed at one end. Five others were put at the opposite end with the piano and toys in between.

As soon as more electrical outlets had been installed, two men set the computers up with the software and they were in business. Since Fausta was computer savvy, she planned to stay in the village for as long as it took to work with each student. She wouldn't leave until they were competent enough to have fun on them without help.

When everything was ready, the Mother Superior took Fausta into the big dining room and introduced her. The children were finishing their dinner. They had no idea who she was or that she'd been the one responsible for the gifts. That was the way Fausta wanted it.

The Mother Superior clapped her hands. "Children? I'd like you to meet Signorina Rossiano. She's the person who is going to show you how to use the computers and printers that were donated to us."

The children shouted with excitement. They attended the local school during the school year and were dying to get their hands on them. Fausta remembered Nico telling her he'd have given anything to work on one.

As she looked at each of the children, she could picture Nico, who'd spent ten years eating meals in this room, and felt a fierce tug on her heart. At the moment there were twenty-nine children from the ages of six to fourteen.

"You'll have to learn how to use them in shifts. Right now we'll start with Emilio, Eva, Nicoletta, Paolo, Sergio, Remo, Teresa, Guido, Maria and Nicolo."

Just hearing that last name caused Fausta's pulse to pick up speed.

"Follow Signorina Rossiano to the common room. Once your turn is over, more of you will be called until everyone has had a chance before it's bedtime."

Teaching the children how to work on the computer turned out to be pure joy for Fausta. She'd never had so much fun in her life.

Since school was out for the summer, she was able to work with the children in shifts throughout the day. They were smart and caught on fast.

* * *

By the following Monday she realized it wouldn't be long before they didn't need her anymore. That put her in a panic. As long as she kept busy, she couldn't agonize openly over Nico until she went to bed.

Fausta decided that when she went back home in a few more days, she would do a fund-raiser to buy more computers and have them installed in other orphanages around Domodossola. Finally she had a cause of her own, separate from Lanza's.

The children's hunger to learn the latest technology convinced her it was a worthy cause in many ways and would help her deal with her pain. But she'd never get over losing Nico. That wasn't possible.

CHAPTER SEVEN

AFTER NICO'S TRIP to La Valazzura, he returned to Domodossola the next Monday morning and drove straight to his office. But this time *he* was the one who had a contingent of bodyguards from La Valazzura following him.

The dozens of messages both on his phone and email account would have to wait. Several were from Felipe and Dr. Silvio. None of them were from Fausta of course.

After working through a full day's schedule of patients, he hurried over to the pediatric ward to find her. Fausta had been burdened with his personal pain and had felt it. He wanted her to know her prayer for him had been answered. His long search to find his parents had been miraculously realized.

If she'd already gone home from the hospital, he'd drive to the palace and wait for as

long as it would take to see her. He'd been
reborn into a new world he had no affinity
for. There was only one person he wanted
to talk to about the tumult going on inside
him and he needed her.

He stopped at the nursing station. "Where
can I find Princess Fausta?"

The nurse looked up. "She's not here. Last
Monday Signorina Vitale told us that the
princess now has a royal commitment that
prevents her from doing any more volunteer
work for the hospital for an indefinite period.
It's a shame because she's the children's favorite person."

That was Nico's fault. Feeling as if he'd
been stabbed, he thanked her and left the
hospital. En route to pick up a quick meal he
phoned Fausta, but could get only her voice
mail. After asking her to call him back immediately, he drove home and went to the
kitchen to make a pot of coffee. He might
be up all night waiting to hear from her and
needed fortification. Maybe he'd done too
much damage and no amount of persuasion
would get her to call him.

Before he'd left the baroque palace in Azzura, he'd made a solemn promise to the
prime minister and Basil. In one month's

time he'd tell them if he wanted to try and fill his father's shoes. But it all depended on the queen. She had yet to consider if she could accept him, let alone back him.

Until he heard from Liliane, Nico needed the next thirty days to do the most serious soul-searching of his life. But he couldn't do any of it without talking to Fausta.

A few minutes after nine his phone rang. He grabbed it. When he saw who was calling, he almost had a heart attack before clicking on. "Fausta?"

"Nico? What kind of emergency would require you to talk to me when we said our goodbyes over a week ago?"

"Something earthshaking. I tried to find you on the pediatric ward and was told you weren't there. You should know that the nurse said they're all in mourning you can't come in to volunteer for a while. You were their favorite."

"That's very kind of her."

"Because it was the truth! Are you still in Rome?"

After a silence she said, "No. Why do you ask?"

"Because I have to see you in person. When will you be back at the palace?"

"Not for a while."

He took a quick breath. "Where are you?"

"Mottalciata."

He rubbed the back of his neck. "What are you doing there?" As if he didn't know.

"I've been here for close to a week doing business with the orphanage."

No doubt having computers installed. She'd said she planned to make it a priority. He stifled a moan. "Where are you staying?"

"At a hotel in the village."

"Which one of the two?"

"Nico—"

"It doesn't matter. I'll find you because I'm coming right now." He hung up and flew out of his apartment after throwing a few necessities into a bag.

Two hours later he drove by the first hotel, trailed by his bodyguards. He saw several cars parked outside. Because one was unmarked, it had to be her bodyguard. He jumped out and hurried inside to the front desk.

But before he could ask the man who'd just come out to the counter to ring her room, Fausta emerged from the staircase, her golden hair flouncing. She had to have been watching for him. With a face and body like hers, she was so gorgeous it took his breath away. She'd dressed in beige pleated pants and a tan colored crew neck top with short sleeves.

"I don't care if it's close to midnight." He spoke first. "I need to talk to you. We can go out to my car or up to your room. The choice is yours."

She rubbed her hands over womanly hips in what he perceived was a nervous reaction. "Follow me."

On the way up to the second floor, he had to stop himself from reaching out to pull her against him. Her room was the second one on the right, adequately furnished with a TV. If the owner downstairs had any idea who she was…

"Sit down, Nico." She indicated one of the chairs at the table before she sat on the other one and crossed one elegant leg over the other. Her suitcase lay open at the end of her bed. Through the bathroom door he could see a robe hanging. The room smelled faintly of her flowery fragrance.

"You look wonderful," he murmured.

"So do you. When I heard this was an emergency, I figured you couldn't have driven here if you were incapacitated. Since

I've worked with children all day and am exhausted, why don't you tell me why you drove here so I can go to bed? I don't think the hotel is full in case you need a room."

"Fausta—I received a call from Enzo. He demanded I cancel the appointments with my patients and come to the *castello*. I couldn't imagine what he wanted, particularly when he insisted it wasn't for medical reasons. When I arrived there the next morning, I found him with a visitor who'd come from La Valazzura to see him."

Her blue eyes flickered. "That's interesting. Papa wanted to fly there for the funeral of King Carlo, a ruler he admired who died recently, but the doctor wouldn't okay it."

Nico couldn't help but wonder if that admiration would influence Fausta's father for good when the truth came out about him. "I'm sorry he didn't get the opportunity." *I'm sorry I didn't either.*

She eyed him steadily. "You haven't told me about your emergency yet."

"The man who visited Enzo was Basil Bruno, the head of the secret service for King Carlo and Queen Liliane."

Her eyebrows furrowed in a gentle frown. "What did he want with Duca Frascatti?"

"He knew Enzo was my mentor."

Fausta sat straighter. "Why did that matter to him?"

This was it. His heart pounded extra hard. "It was Signor Bruno who placed me in the Santa'Agate Orphanage when I was two."

A cry escaped her lips.

"My legal name is Massimo. During the beginning of their civil war, I was taken to safety and am the only living son of King Carlo Umberto Fernando di Savoia."

The world stood still for a minute.

"Nico—" Her gasp filled the room.

"For the last week I've been in La Valazzura learning as much about the lives of my parents and my heritage as I could absorb before flying back. You were the one person I wanted to see, but you weren't at the hospital. I never meant to hurt you. It killed me to learn you'd stopped volunteering because of me."

"None of that matters." She wiped her wet face with the backs of her hands. "Nothing is as important as knowing that in the last week you've found your life! You have answers to all your questions. There couldn't be a greater gift! You're the son of King

Carlo? How absolutely fantastic. Who would have imagined?"

"Certainly not Angelo."

"No," she said with a laugh as more tears escaped her lashes.

"Especially when he learns I'm the *illegitimate* son."

The smile slowly faded from her face. "What do you mean?"

"My father betrayed the queen during a bad time in their marriage. They could never have children. He had an affair with my mamma, who was a commoner. Her name was Nedda Corelli."

"Oh, no," she half groaned. "Did you spend time with her?"

"That would have been impossible. She was killed during the war that swept the country. To preserve my life, I was taken to the orphanage in secret by Signor Bruno."

Fausta got up from the chair and came to kneel in front of him. "I'm crushed you never did get to meet either parent." She grasped his hands, lifting those iridescent blue eyes to him. "Do you wish you'd never found out about your life?"

After a long pause he said, "Basil asked

me the same question. I told him I didn't
know how to answer him. I still don't."

She let go of his hands and got up to sit on
the side of the bed. "That's because you're
grieving over the parents you never got to
know."

"It's more than that, Fausta. Every time
Queen Liliane looks at me, she's torn apart
all over again, hating the horrible truth that
her husband had carried on an affair with my
mother. I'm the son who should have been
Liliane's. It's a monstrous scenario."

"I agree," Fausta said in a quiet voice,
"and I can't imagine her pain or yours. But
if you will look beyond it for a moment, you
now know who you are and where you came
from. You don't have to go through the rest
of your life wondering and waiting."

He stared into her eyes. She was making
sense. "That's true."

"After I flew to Rome to be with my *zia*
Ottavia, I unloaded on her. As we talked, I
began to realize it was selfish of me to be
hurt by your decision that we end our relationship. All these years you've been on a
journey that needed to be taken alone. I understand that better now. I'll admit I didn't
like it, but I refused to wallow in my pain

and decided to concentrate on helping the orphanage."

There was no one like Fausta. "So you don't mind my trying to reach you tonight?"

Her chest rose and fell visibly. "I would *never* have forgiven you if you hadn't." The fierceness of her tone convinced him she'd meant it. "What's going to happen now?"

Nico got up from the chair and walked around for a minute before turning to her. "Since my parents have died and are buried, I can go on with my life being a doctor here in Domodossola."

She lifted her head to look at him, but her sober expression gave no indication of what was going on inside her. "Or?" she prodded. "You're being pressured to become the next king."

Fausta hadn't grown up the daughter of a king for nothing. "I've been approached by Basil and the prime minister to consider it."

"That isn't surprising. A while back at breakfast I remember Papa saying how tragic it was that there was no son to inherit the throne of La Valazzura."

"Your father spoke the truth. Unfortunately, it's criminal that the only one is the bastard love child who is infinitely unqualified to be the head of the country."

"I don't know." A smile broke out on her beautiful face. "You've been a pig farmer. That has to count with all the farmers who need their king to understand the industry that feeds its citizens."

"Be serious, Fausta."

"I'm being very serious. You're a doctor at a time when health care is the chief concern of every head of state on earth. No one could know more about it than you. For that matter, who could dictate immigration policies or understand the plight of war-torn orphans and refugees of this world better than a king who'd grown up in an orphanage to survive?"

"Fausta…"

"It's true. The more I think about it, I can't conceive of a man in today's world who would suit the demands facing your country more than you do."

He scoffed, though he was deeply touched by her words. "You forget the faction of government that didn't like my father's policies. There's a cousin of my father's, Giuseppe Umberto, who started the war thirty years ago and is waging a campaign to be put in as king by the parliament."

"There's always an opposition party with someone overly zealous and ready to take over. Does this Giuseppe know you exist?"

"I'm afraid he does now."

"How does the queen feel about it?"

"I have no idea. She hasn't had enough time to get over the shock that I'm alive."

"You mean she didn't know?"

"She knew there'd been a child but thought I had died too. She was never told I'd been taken to safety. When Basil walked me in to the palace to meet her, she took one look at me and almost fainted. There's a strong resemblance between me and my father. I'll show you."

He pulled four photos from his breast pocket and handed them to her. Two of them were the ones Basil had given him. The other two were of his father, one when he was older, the other just before he died.

As she studied them, she shook her head. "How utterly incredible! You don't need a DNA test. No wonder the queen went into shock." Fausta kept scrutinizing them. "Your mother was so lovely. There's a look around her eyes that reminds me of you. How hard

for you that you never got to know them."
She put the photos on the bed. "I don't know
what to say," she murmured in a tearful
voice.

"I'm afraid that's *my* dilemma."

"Of course it is—" she cried with infinite
understanding.

Nico needed to hold her more than he
needed life itself. In the next instant he
reached for her. They clung to each other
before he found her mouth and began kissing the daylights out of her. Tonight he'd discovered she was his rock.

"I've missed you so terribly, Nico."

"Tell me about it." Their need for each
other was off the charts. He couldn't get
enough of her. "You've got to stop me,
Fausta. I need to go downstairs and get a
room. I was assigned bodyguards before I
left La Valazzura. Combined with yours, our
every move is being watched."

She kissed his features. "Now you're
going to find out what it's like to be royal.
I've always hated it, Nico."

"Understood," he whispered. "What an
irony of ironies," he said against her lus-
cious mouth before devouring her all over
again. His need for her was out of control

and always had been since the evening they went to Prospero's. But eventually he was forced to call on every atom of self-control to let her go.

"In the morning I'll come by your room and we'll go to breakfast before driving over to the orphanage. I want to see what magic you've performed."

Fausta hugged him harder. "I don't want you to leave."

"You think *I* do?" His voice shook. "But I know we can't do this right now. Too much is at stake, above all your reputation."

She made a sound of exasperation and eased out of his arms. "I've told you before that I'm not concerned about what my parents want."

"I'm afraid I am."

Her expression closed up. "You're thinking like a royal already."

He shook his head. "I'm thinking you and I have a lot to talk about in the next thirty days."

"Why thirty days?"

Nico let out a troubled sigh. "That's when I have to let Signor Bruno and the prime minister know if I've decided to return to La Valazzura and take on my father's mantle."

"I see."

"The queen will have to be in agreement before I'm presented to the parliament for a vote. Even then Giuseppe could be the one who prevails in that fight. Until then, all options are on the table. Now I need to get out of here before I can't!"

Fausta couldn't stand it to watch him tear out of her hotel room, but she had no choice. If he only knew he'd left her so unsatisfied physically, she was in pain and clung to the back of one of the chairs for support.

What did he mean that all options were on the table? There were only two. Either he remained a doctor in Domodossola, or he embraced his destiny in La Valazzura.

She spent the rest of the night in absolute turmoil. When he'd driven here to see her, she'd thought he'd come to tell her he was in love with her and wanted to marry her. If he never found his parents it didn't matter, because he didn't want to continue his journey without her. And if one day he did get the information he'd been looking for, Fausta would be with him and the future would take care of itself.

Together they'd fight any opposition from

her parents and settle down in an adorable house with a picket fence and children. They'd be a married couple with a whole life ahead of them until circumstances changed for them. Fausta had gone crazy waiting for him to show up at the hotel so she could tell him she loved him more than life itself.

Nothing in a million years could have prepared her for his astounding news after he arrived. It was one thing to learn he'd found his parents. But to be told he was the undeclared, beloved son and heir of King Carlo Umberto of La Valazzura had turned her inside out.

The noble part of the orphaned boy engrained inside Nico would be overjoyed and want to honor his father by following in his footsteps. Everything that had happened to him in his life until the arrival of Signor Bruno had been a preparation. Fausta believed it and had pointed those things out to him because she knew he'd already made the decision in his heart.

But *her* heart wasn't in it. How could it be when she'd wished she hadn't been born a royal? The restrictive life had brought her little pleasure. At Enrico's coronation, Fausta had told Donetta she planned to marry a commoner and nothing would ever change her mind. Her sister had replied, "Be careful what you wish for."

A shiver racked her body now.

In making that wish, the commoner she'd fallen head over heels in love with had turned out to be the son of a king. She couldn't be happy about it, not for him or for herself.

With this knowledge, Fausta's world had forever changed because Nico would always be the love of her life. But sadness had enveloped her because he wasn't who she thought he was. It changed everything.

Fausta tried to shake off her sadness as they drove over to the orphanage after eating at a trattoria. She had to keep reminding herself that this entire situation was about him, not her. It was beyond selfish of her to feel this torn up.

He'd achieved the goal in his life to find out who he was and where he came from. But when she'd fallen madly in love with him, little did she realize what rivers of sorrow she would have to cross as a result.

When they arrived at the orphanage, the children were out in the back courtyard playing. Nico followed Fausta inside.

"What do you think?" She was anxious to know his reaction.

He walked into the common room with her, dressed in a linen shirt and khaki trousers. She found him so handsome, it hurt.

After looking at all the equipment and their placement, he whistled. "The room has been transformed." One of the nuns had set up a mobile bulletin board on wheels with a lot of pictures the children had run off on the printers. They'd signed their names. Fausta watched him study each one.

"*Ehi!* Here's a robot designed by my namesake."

Fausta smiled. "Nicolo is a cute little seven-year-old redhead who is crazy about everything related to the computer and doesn't want to do anything else. Maybe he'll be a big tech genius one day."

Nico raised his eyes to her, enveloping her with heat. "You'll be the reason why. I can't tell you how impressed I am. You're a wonder."

Her pulse raced. "It has been so much fun to teach the children. They're smart and have learned fast. I should have become an elementary school teacher."

He moved toward her. "Why didn't you?"

"That's not the kind of thing one of my father's daughters is allowed to do."

A frown marred his striking features. "How much longer are you planning to stay here?"

"Today's my last day."

"The place will fall apart without you."

She chuckled. "Oh, no. The nuns have been learning too, and they help the children."

"It won't be the same."

"You're right. I'll miss them terribly, but not for long."

"What do you mean?"

"As soon as I get back to Domodossola, I'm going to make visits to the various orphanages. I have no idea how many exist. When I've done my homework, I'm going to set up new fund-raisers and use the proceeds to buy more computers and printers. It's going to be my project from here on out. All children are hungry to learn."

Suddenly a whole group of children came running in the room and hurried to the computers.

"Children? Before you get started, I'd like you to meet Dr. Barsotti. He used to live here at the orphanage too."

"For how long?" asked Teresa.

"Ten years," Nico answered.

"Did you get adopted?"

The unexpected question touched her to the core. She could only imagine how Nico felt at this point.

"No. Still, I had several good friends who watched out for me. But we never had computers or a teacher like Signorina Rossiano."

"She's not a nun," Sergio blurted.

Nico grinned. "Is that good or bad?"

"Good. She's fun!"

"You're right." Nico's eyes wandered over her. "Your teacher is not only fun, she has the sweetest nature of anyone I've ever known."

Heat swept into her cheeks. "Children? Dr. Barsotti is a good friend," Fausta interjected. "We're here to help you learn how to cut and paste." She darted him an impish glance. "Shall we get started?"

He got right into it with her and was too wonderful. After two hours had passed, she made the announcement to this first group that today would be her last day with them. "But I'll be back to check on you in another month."

She hadn't forgotten what Nico had told

her about orphan institutions where the staff had large turnovers. She was already starting to feel a bond with these children. Fausta would love to adopt all of them.

"How come you have to go?"

"So I can help at other orphanages, Maria."

"Oh."

One of the nuns escorted the children from the room. Then another group came running in and the whole routine began again. By five in the afternoon she'd said goodbye to the last session. The second they disappeared out the door, she buried her face in her hands, overcome with emotion.

Nico's arms came around her from behind. He buried his face in her hair. "I wouldn't have missed this day for the world. You've touched their lives and they'll never forget you."

"They've touched mine." She wiped her eyes and turned around. "Thank you for helping. To see you working with the children when you were once a resident here…"

She couldn't finish what she was going to say because his mouth covered hers. He kissed her with so much hunger, she forgot where they were and wanted it to go on forever.

"Signorina Rossiano?"

Fausta pulled away from him, embarrassed to be caught in his arms.

Maria, the eight-year-old with the long dark hair, had come in the room. "I wish you didn't have to go." She ran over to hug her around the waist.

"I don't want to, but I'll see you again before summer is over."

"Do you promise?"

"I promise." She kissed her forehead before the girl left the room.

"Oh, Nico—"

He put his arm around her shoulders. "Come on. Let's leave for the hotel and freshen up. Then we'll go out for dinner in Biella. Afterward we'll go back to the hotel. It will give us time to talk before we return to Domodossola in the morning."

CHAPTER EIGHT

Nico sat back in the chair to drink his wine while he feasted his eyes on Fausta in the candlelight. Could any woman be more gorgeous?

"I remember passing this *ristorante* when I explored Biella for the first time at the age of fourteen. So many finely dressed people sat out on this patio eating foods I'd never dreamed of. They didn't seem to have a care in the world. I couldn't comprehend living their lives."

She flashed him a sad smile. "And soon, other teenage boys in La Valazzura will see their new king riding through the city in a carriage after his coronation. They won't be able to comprehend *your* world."

Her words disturbed him. He put his half-empty glass on the table. "You think I've made my decision already?"

"Haven't you?" Fausta was always direct. That was one of the many qualities he loved about her. "Your parents may no longer be alive, but your legacy is there waiting for you."

"I'm not at all sure about that."

Those blue eyes studied him intently. "I remember your telling me that if you found out your parents were from Domodossola, you would stay. But if you found them elsewhere, their country would be your country and you would put down roots. I happen to know you meant those words with all your heart."

Nico groaned softly. "I didn't count on another woman being tormented that I'm alive."

She cocked her head. "In all honesty, the queen *did* know about the affair. At this point you must have some idea how she feels about you deep inside."

"It doesn't help that I look so much like my father. Try to put yourself in her place."

He could hear her mind working. "Were they in love in the beginning, or was it a marriage of convenience?"

"Their marriage was arranged, but in time they fell in love. Basil confirmed it was a happy marriage until they realized there would be no children."

After a prolonged silence she said, "If that's true, and then he had an affair..." She shook her head. "If that had happened to me, it would have killed me and any love I'd had for him. I would have gone away and asked for a divorce. I'm afraid I know myself too well. It would destroy me to see the child of their love ascend the throne when I couldn't have a baby with him."

"That's what I thought you'd say."

She leaned forward and grasped his hand. "I'm sorry, Nico. I didn't mean to hurt you."

"You've only spoken the truth, Fausta, and that's what I want. In order to counteract my pain, both Basil and the prime minister have told me what a great man he was. But to do that to his wife... Far be it from me to judge any man, but—"

"But he *was* your father," she broke in with heartfelt emotion. "You wanted to love who he was, whatever his faults. He was the man you'd idolized somewhere in your psyche without knowing anything about him."

"Your understanding is a revelation to me, Fausta. It isn't just my father I'd ascribed with numberless virtues. How could my own mother have brought herself to get involved with a married man?"

"Then you believe she knew he was the king?"

He nodded. "Liliane told me all about it. They'd been fighting because she wanted to adopt and he was adamant that he didn't want to raise someone else's child. During that difficult period, he left to make visits to several military cemeteries across the country and honor fallen heroes. It was in winter and he came down with the flu that caused him to collapse."

"Oh, no."

"My father was taken to the hospital in Mesecino and had to stay down for close to a week. A young nurse took care of him. As soon as she could, Liliane rushed to his side. But the moment she entered his hospital room, she knew something had happened. My father was more distant, and it became clear he and the nurse had become involved."

"That story is too painful," Fausta whispered.

Nico agreed. "Liliane said the clandestine affair lasted for about a year before he came to her and confessed to everything, including the fact that they'd had a baby son. By then full war had broken out."

A moan came out of the woman seated across from him.

"He begged Liliane's forgiveness for his weakness, insisting that he loved her and always would. He also promised he would never see my mother or the baby again and kept that promise, although he made provisions for them to be taken care of through Basil. My father did keep his promise to Liliane, but nothing was ever the same between them."

"No. It couldn't be. So what are you saying, Nico?"

He finished his wine. "Basil and the prime minister want me to take my place as the heir apparent to the throne and believe the parliament would be behind me. They insist the queen has no vote politically and couldn't stop me. But I told them that if she can't get past her pain—and I don't see how she can—then there's no way I would consider murdering her heart again. My father already did it once."

"Nico—please don't let what I said influence you in any way."

"You didn't. I was sickened the moment Liliane spoke frankly with me. I left La Valazzura with this proviso: unless I hear from Liliane herself before the thirty days are up, and she can see a path for me that wouldn't destroy her, then I'd think about it. The palace is her home since she left her father's palace in Slovenia years ago to be married. For the time being she's a figurehead no matter who ascends the throne."

"That poor woman. My heart aches for her." Fausta's head lifted. "My heart aches for *you*. I wish I could take away your pain."

"You already have by just being you. I needed this day with you and am looking forward to getting back to work as long as you're free at five o'clock every day and weekends for us to be together. Once you tell your parents the truth about me, they might even add me to the bottom rung of their short list of acceptables."

Nico thought she would smile, but the opposite was true. "Do you mind if we go back to the hotel?"

"I didn't mean to say the wrong thing."

She refused to look at him. "You didn't, but I'd rather continue the rest of this conversation when we don't have an audience."

Several people had probably recognized her. "Would you like dessert?"

"I couldn't, but please order for yourself."

"I'd rather be alone with you." He paid the bill and they left the restaurant for the car.

When he pulled in next to her car in the hotel parking lot, he turned to her. "Why did my mentioning your parents bother you so much?"

"I'd rather not talk about it."

"Fausta—you and I don't have secrets from each other. I don't want to start now."

She suddenly looked at him. Her eyes glittered with unshed tears. "I've spent my life wishing I weren't royal so I could be like all my friends, able to make choices without worrying about the royal rules governing what my parents have outlined for me. I've said it before, the difference between the classes is indecent."

"I'm aware of how you feel," he whispered.

"Do you have any idea how strange it is to hear you of all people say that you're probably acceptable to my parents now that you have a pedigree that goes back thousands of years? It angers me when I think of how Angelo spoke to you about crossing lines. No human should have to worry about being good enough to associate with another human."

"Fausta…" He pulled her to him and kissed the tears off her cheeks.

"After that lovely dinner, I'm sorry for being so upset, Nico. Forgive me, but so many things pain me. I wish you could enjoy your parents' love story. They must have been attracted to the point they couldn't deny themselves. How hard it must have been for them to part. He never got to see you again." She buried her face in his neck and wept quietly.

"I'm presuming it was even harder to face his wife with the truth while continuing to rule," Nico murmured. "I'm glad I knew nothing until now."

She raised her head and looked into his eyes. "Thank heaven you were taken to safety! Your parents would be so proud of you if they knew what an amazing man you've become. Maybe they do know."

"*Bellissima—*" Nico embraced her harder.

Fausta ran her hand through his hair. "Isn't it amazing that after all the searches you made and would continue to make throughout your life, it was Basil who came to you with the information only he could have provided? Does he know if your mother still has relatives living? It's possible you have aunts and uncles who might be able to tell you more about her."

He took a deep breath. "We didn't have time to talk about that yet. He and the prime minister tried to cram a hundred years' worth of their country's history into my brain over those five days."

"I can imagine. What about your father's family?"

"Aside from the cousin I told you about, all the relatives have passed on due to the ravages of war."

"I realize I'm brimming with so many questions, it's driving you crazy."

"I love it, otherwise I wouldn't have driven here the second I flew home. I need you to help me make sense of everything. Let's go back to your room. We have all night to be together before leaving for Domodossola in the morning."

"That wouldn't be a good idea, and I'm not talking about our bodyguards keeping watch. I don't trust myself alone with you, so it's better if we talk here in the car."

When she tried to ease away from him, he wouldn't let her go. "Don't you know how much I want you? You have no idea how I've longed for you."

"Your father probably told your mother the same thing before they lost their heads. Look what happened! Their lives were ripped apart. You and I can't afford to do the same thing."

"You're not making sense."

"Oh, yes, I am. Anything could happen in the next thirty days. I'm convinced you'll hear from the queen. She loved your father once. In the end she'll want you to return to La Valazzura and go before the parliament endowed with the many qualities that made him a great king even my own father admired."

"Then you have a lot more faith than I do."

"Please listen, Nico. Don't you know how tragic it would it be for Basil and the prime minister to receive a message that the still unwed Princess Rossiano of Domodossola is the mistress of the commoner-turned-uncrowned-king before the throne is even his? The people would fear a potential pregnancy. If you can't imagine it, I can. *Like father, like son. It must run in the genes.*

The press will go ballistic with glee and tear you apart."

"Don't," Nico begged and crushed her to him. "Surely by now you know how deeply I'm in love with you."

"Actually I *don't* know," she fired back, her face awash in tears. "You couldn't tell me how you feel until now because you didn't dare say the words to a princess. Angelo really got to you. You've always felt you didn't deserve to be with me. But now that you've found your life and we're equals, you're suddenly entitled to speak those forbidden words of love?"

"Fausta—" He tried to kiss her, but she wouldn't let him.

"Do you have any idea how much I needed to hear you say you loved me when we were at your apartment, *before* you knew who you were? I would have done anything for you. But you couldn't say the words. That's why a relationship based on what we've had up to now is thin as air."

"Don't talk that way, *amore mio*."

"Nico, we've spent borrowed time together for a short while. You believed it had to end and broke up with me that night at your apartment, telling me you were on a search for your parents that had to be taken alone. The real reason was that you couldn't see us ending up together. I thought I was going to die and couldn't believe I was still alive the next day."

He smoothed the moisture off her cheeks. "You'll never know what I went through."

"Does it matter? When you leave for La Valazzura, and I know you will, a royal world will await you complete with a list of princesses dying to meet you. At that point all things will be equal. You'll have the time you need to find the right woman for you, one who will hold your heart and give you children. There'll be no baggage and you'll be a revered king."

"Listen to me, Fausta. You're the woman who holds my heart. I want children with you and no one else. Whether I become a king or remain a doctor, there's no one else in this world for me but you."

She shook her head. "I believe you mean it, but you're a man suspended high between two worlds. I'm watching in agony from below."

"*Mia amata—*" He cupped her face in his hands and kissed her with such passion they were both breathless. "Whatever world

I choose, I need the answer to one question. Will you marry me?"

Nico reached in his pocket and pulled out a ring. "This is a blue diamond, close to the color of your eyes. I bought this after we spent that day in the country together. Tonight, I intended to give it to you. That's how real my love has been for you from the beginning."

A gasp escaped her lips. He felt for her left hand, but she wouldn't cooperate. "I—I can't accept it," she stammered.

"In the name of heaven, why not? Have you decided you don't love me?"

Her cry resonated in the interior of the car. "Don't be ridiculous. I'm so in love with you, I've been half out of my mind since the first evening you took me to dinner."

"Then why won't you let me put it on you?"

She threw her head back. "If you were the doctor from the hospital asking me to spend the rest of my life with you, I would put it on myself and never take it off. But you're not Nico Barsotti. Your name is Massimo Carlo Umberto, the future king of La Valazzura, and you're going to have a remarkable reign."

"You don't know that!" he cried in frustration. "Hell, I don't even know what I'm feeling yet."

"You're still too close to it, but I feel it in my bones. Unlike you, I've known who I was and have known my own feelings from the time I was a young girl. I knew I was a loved princess who had to sit still for the royal family pictures and wait all the time to see my father for a few minutes. I didn't like that life then, and I don't like it now. I want to marry a man with a normal life like the magnificent family practice doctor I fell so hard for."

"Fausta—"

"When you fixed dinner for us in your apartment, I thought you were going to propose to me. I'd been picturing our life together. I even went so far in my thoughts to imagine that if we couldn't have children because either one of us had a problem, we'd go to the orphanage and adopt a little Nicolo or Maria. The dreams I've had…"

She pressed her lips to his. "Those dreams will keep me warm in my old age. Years from tonight I'll remember that the great king of La Valazzura once asked me to marry him. And now I'm going to say good-night and goodbye. Please don't see me inside the hotel or call me. I need to be by myself."

"What am I going to do, Enzo?"

Nico had driven to the *castello* on Wednesday morning after watching Fausta leave the hotel in her car. He hadn't slept all night. His heart had gone with her, leaving him in agony.

His white-haired mentor eyed him with a solemn expression after Nico had poured out his soul to him. "I wish I could help. The only advice I have for you is that you don't make your decision hastily then live a lifetime of regret if it's the wrong one."

"That's my biggest worry. I only have a month before I must act one way or the other. There are so many unknowns, Enzo. Fausta has brought me the greatest happiness I've ever known. Whatever I do, there can be no joy in my life without her. She lights up my world and everyone else's."

"Indeed she does," Pippa chimed in. "Even as a girl she had a spirit and vivaciousness we noticed immediately. According to Lorenzo, she's been a worry to her parents because she's not biddable like her sisters and has rebelled over being a royal. She knows her own mind."

Nico clung to the back of a damask chair, unable to sit. "She made that painfully clear last night when she refused the ring I bought her."

Enzo sighed. "Fausta is Victor's daughter and wise beyond her years. Not only has she shown her superb taste in falling for you, she has learned the lesson of not jumping into the fire too soon. Give her time to assimilate what you've told her."

"If you'd heard her last night, you'd know there's no hope."

Pippa smiled at him. "There's always hope when there's love."

"I've got to pray you're right, Pippa."

"Don't forget she's been imagining being the wife of a doctor at the risk of estranging her parents. She's been comfortable with that idea and has figured out how she's going to keep you close to her so the two of you can have a wonderful life together. But now you've thrown her a huge curve."

"A royal curve she doesn't like," Enzo concurred.

Pippa wheeled herself closer. "Fausta needs time to get used to the fact that you might become king of another country, one foreign to both of you."

"I'm still having trouble comprehending it."

"Just remember that she has watched her mother deal with being her father's queen since she was a toddler. I believe her fear stems from a lot more than living a royal life with you if she has to."

"What do you mean?"

"Fausta has been there and done that while she too has been forced to wait for her father's attention. It's no mystery why she has grown up wanting marriage with a man who comes home from work to her at five every evening."

Pippa's comment were beginning to make sense.

"What terrifies her most is that the two of you will rarely have time together when you're king. Over the years she has watched her mother waiting, waiting, waiting for those precious times to be alone with her husband. I can't say I blame Fausta for dreading that same scenario for herself."

"Pippa's right, *mio figlio.* So be patient while Fausta starts working out how she as queen can get you to herself more often and keep you in love with her."

"I'll love her beyond life," Nico ground out.

"I believe you will," Enzo murmured. "What's your plan at the moment?"

"To get back to the hospital. Dr. Silvio has doubled for me and I owe him. If or when I hear from Queen Liliane, that will help determine how I proceed."

Nico's white-haired mentor eyed him with a solemn expression. "I wish I could help. Once again, the only advice I have for you is that you weigh your decision carefully. But when you only have a month before you must act one way or the other, that sounds ridiculous, doesn't it?"

"Above all, don't leave Fausta alone," Pippa added. "No matter what she said, she really doesn't want you to stay away from her. You do understand that in her heart, the sun rises and sets with you. I saw it while the two of you were here."

"I want to believe that, Pippa." He walked around and kissed them both. "What would I have done without you two? All the time I was looking for my parents, I had you. I've been blessed. The second I know anything,

I'll drive here to give you checkups and we'll talk. Stay well. I need you."

He left the *castello* for Domodossola. All the way to his apartment he pondered their remarks and advice.

Don't give up on me, Fausta. Per l'amor di Dio, *don't give up.*

CHAPTER NINE

FAUSTA CRIED SO hard all the way back to Domodossola, her blouse was soaked with tears and her face looked ravaged.

When she reached the palace, she swept past the guard on the way up to the apartment with her suitcase. There were eight text messages on her cell phone she'd ignored while she'd been driving home.

Adrenaline gushed through her body when she saw that four of them were from Nico sent at various intervals. She sank down on the side of the bed in pain. Fausta had said goodbye to him and she'd meant it.

At first she couldn't look at them, but finally she caved and read the first one.

I love you, Fausta. It happened when I walked into Tommaso's hospital room and heard you reading to him.

Tears dripped down her cheeks. She read the second one.

We were meant to be together. I felt it when we visited the orphanage the first time and know you felt it too.

Fausta's heartache deepened and she jumped off the bed before reading the third one.

I'll never say goodbye to you, so don't think you're going to get rid of me. That wouldn't be possible.

"Nico—" she cried out in anguish and pressed the phone to her chest. But the last message was still calling to her. With trembling fingers, she opened it.

Fausta. I meant it when I said you were the only woman for me. From the very first moment you spoke to my heart. That only happens once in a lifetime. I'm not giving up, so be warned.

Completely torn up inside, she needed her sister and phoned her.

Lanza had just put Rufy down for his afternoon nap and said she'd come right away.

The second she knocked and walked in, Fausta ran to her and they hugged.

"Tell me what's wrong. You sounded frantic on the phone."

"There's so much to tell you, I don't know where to start."

"This is about Nico I'm sure."

She nodded. They ended up on the couch in her sitting room. "What I'm about to tell you can't go beyond these walls."

Lanza's brows lifted. "It's that bad?"

"It is for me."

"Fausta—don't keep me in suspense."

"All right. Here it is. Nico was put in an orphanage at the age of two and was never adopted, though he'd had two opportunities. The point is, a little more than a week ago he found out where he came from and who his parents are."

By now she had Lanza's complete attention. "Was his mother a single mom who couldn't take care of him?"

"No." Fausta twisted her fingers together. "She was a young nurse in Mesecino, La Valazzura, who took care of a man in the hospital with a virus. They fell in love and had an affair. It turns out Nico's real name is Massimo Carlo Umberto Fernando, the only son of King Carlo di Savoia."

Lanza's eyes widened. "King Carlo who died recently?"

"The very one."

"Dr. Barsotti is his son?"

"The illegitimate son. King Carlo and his wife, Queen Liliane, couldn't have children. Nedda Corelli was Nico's mother and the king's mistress, but she died during the war over there when Nico was only two."

Too late Lanza tried to cover a gasp with her hand.

For the next few minutes Fausta told her his history, the reason he'd been put in an orphanage, everything. She included the fact that the prime minister and the head of the secret service wanted him to go before the parliament as the heir apparent.

"They're convinced he'll be voted in and crowned king in his father's stead. But he'll only agree with the queen's approval because he recognizes her deep pain."

"Good heavens, Fausta!" Her sister got to her feet. "This is all unbelievable! So, if she can get past her pain, Dr. Barsotti will be the next king of La Valazzura."

Fausta looked up at her through the tears. "Yes. Here I thought I'd found the man I'd been wishing for all my life. Instead he has turned out to be the one thing I never wanted."

Her sister eyed her intently. "Has he asked you to marry him?"

"Yes, but only after he found out he was the son of King Carlo."

"Come on, Fausta. You know why. That's because he didn't dare ask you to marry him believing you're destined to marry some prince. The media has talked nonstop about your royal future."

Her jaw hardened. "Do you have any idea how angry that makes me feel? I told him I couldn't marry him and refused the diamond ring he tried to give me. He said he bought it after our first trip to Biella, but he didn't propose then."

"*What?* You mean he bought you a ring before he knew about his heritage? Are you crazy to turn down such a courageous act when you're madly in love with him?"

"I don't want to marry royalty. You more than anyone in this world besides Donetta know how I feel about that."

Her sister frowned. "I'm afraid I do. But

this particular king happens to be the man you adore."

Fausta swallowed hard. "I know. I was an idiot."

"I think it's destiny. The parents will be overjoyed when they find out. I know for a fact they'll give you their blessing. Papa holds Nico's father in high esteem. He talked about him at breakfast."

"I remember, but that doesn't help my situation. I'll be sitting in a palace for the rest of my born days while Nico runs the country and manages to eke out a little time for me." Fausta got to her feet. "No, thank you. I'd rather remain single."

"Don't forget there'll be children."

"Don't forget that Stefano lets you travel with him when he has to go to the gold mines. I envy you that."

Lanza reached for her hand. "Come and sit down with me again." Fausta did her bidding. "Tell me something. When you found out that Nico was an orphan, did that make you love him less or more?"

"I—I don't know how to answer that." Her voice faltered. "I admit that I admired him for making such a success of his life, but I fell in love with him at the very beginning and didn't care about anything else."

"Since you loved him not knowing anything about his birth parents and background, then it meant you accepted him just as he was, an orphan who became a busy doctor. So now that you've found out he's the son of a king, why does that make a difference?

"He loves you and wants you to marry him. Isn't your love more important than what he's going to do in the future as long you're with him?" Lanza used her brilliant logic to get to the heart of the matter in a hurry.

"I don't know."

"As I recall, you've always maintained that marrying a commoner would make a marriage between the two of you more interesting. Remember that he *was* a commoner until just a week or two ago. Learning that he's a future king really spices up your whole relationship. Think about that for a while before you push the greatest love you'll ever know out of your life. That kind of love only comes once in a lifetime."

A shiver passed through Fausta's body. Nico had texted those exact words to her.

Lanza kissed her cheek. "I love you and know you'll work it all out. Now I have to get back to Rufy."

"Bless you for listening to me."

When her sister disappeared, Fausta walked around, trying to come to grips with what Lanza had just said. But her sister had been kind about it.

What she'd really implied was that Fausta was being selfish, always dreaming about what she wanted. She expected Nico to stay in Domodossola for her sake when the life he was born to happened to mean he was the uncrowned Prince of La Valazzura. The orphan boy was the son of a wonderful king. Nico could also do great good for his country and honor his legacy.

Yet he *had* dared to love her! He'd let her into his life and had told her all his secrets. He'd fought for her. He'd declared his love and had even bought her a ring he probably believed wouldn't be good enough for her. And what had she'd done? Thrown it all back in his unforgettably striking face.

When she put herself in Nico's place, she realized that in rejecting him, she'd done the worst thing anyone could do. To expect so much of him would mean holding him back from his destiny if he wanted to follow in his father's footsteps.

Throughout the rest of the afternoon Fausta did a lot of soul-searching. By evening she was done with tears and realized that life without him was no life at all.

She checked her watch. By now he was probably on his way home from the hospital. Though she could phone him, that wouldn't be enough. She needed to see him face-to-face and tell him how much she loved him, beg his forgiveness for the way she'd been reacting. He needed to know all the secrets of her heart she'd kept from him.

After she took a shower and dressed in a sleeveless white sundress, she left the palace and drove to his apartment in the other part of town. On the way she picked up some food at her favorite deli for them to enjoy.

Since she knew his car, she parked along the street and would wait until she spotted him, then follow him inside. Fausta was sick with excitement and running a fever at the thought of being with him. Once she got her arms around him, she'd never let him go.

Nico's last patient didn't leave until ten after six p.m. He had half a dozen calls to return, but he'd make them after he drove home. He'd texted Fausta during the drive to Domodossola and didn't expect to hear from her. But he was following Pippa's advice and wouldn't leave her alone.

Tomorrow night he planned to drive over to the palace and call her from outside her private entrance. He'd keep after her until she responded. These thoughts and more filled his mind as he reached the parking area of his apartment and hurried inside.

It was a hot night. No sooner had he gone into the kitchen for a cold glass of water than he heard a knock on the door. That was a surprise. Maybe it was Felipe.

He hurried to the door and came close to going into cardiac arrest to see Fausta standing there in all her golden glory. She held a sack in one hand, her purse in the other. In that filmy white dress with the spaghetti straps, he thought he'd never seen anyone so breathtaking.

"Nico—" Her anxious blue eyes searched his. "Will you forgive me for bursting in on you like this? I was sitting out in my car waiting for you to come home. I brought dinner if you want some, but if you'd rather be alone—"

"Come here to me." He pulled her inside. In an instant he relieved her of the purse and sack, then picked her up in his arms and carried her over to the couch. She half lay against him as he hungrily covered her mouth with his own.

Nico no longer had cognizance of time or surroundings. The fire that had been kindling over the weeks burst into flame. Her kisses intoxicated him. She held nothing back.

"I love you more than you'll ever know, Nico. I want to be your wife," she cried breathlessly. "Forgive me for being so cruel to you."

He lifted his head. "Cruel?"

"Yes, my darling. I'm ashamed of the way I've treated you. I've had issues and hang-ups about my life as a royal and I've let them come close to ruining my relationship with you."

"What's made you change since last night?"

"Lanza."

"I don't understand."

"Today she asked me a few salient questions that made me realize what a selfish creature I've been."

Nico burst into laughter. "I've never known anyone less selfish than you."

She shifted in his arms so she could look into his eyes. "That's because you don't know the real me. Since I met you, I've wanted everything my way. When I found out you were the son of a king, I hated it. I wasn't thinking about you and how ecstatic you were to have found your parents and your roots.

"Oh, no. I was only thinking of myself and how that knowledge affected me. I desired the fictional man I'd dreamed about all my life. A commoner. He'd take me to his cottage with a picket fence. We'd have perfect children and live a blissful life. The first time I saw you, I knew you were the man of my dreams, and I set out to capture you no matter what I had to do."

"You accomplished your objective." Nico kissed her long and hard. This was the warm, giving woman he adored.

Tears smarted her eyelids. "I can't believe I didn't accept the ring when you asked me to marry you. I was so entrenched with my own pitiful vision of royal life, I ruined what should have been the most magical, thrilling moment of our lives. I don't know why you didn't slam the door in my face a little while ago."

He kissed her throat. "I have a confession of my own. On my way home, I stopped to talk to Enzo and Pippa. They told me I had to give you time. I've been hanging on to their advice for dear life."

"They're wise and wonderful. So is Lanza. I wish it hadn't taken the questions she asked me for me to wake up and realize what a fool I've been. Oh, Nico. Please tell me it's not too late." She put her arms around his neck. "I love you with every breath of my body. I don't care what you do for a living as long as I'm there with you. We'll make it work."

"You're reading my mind." Nico reached in the front pocket of his trousers and pulled out the ring. He found her left hand and slid it home on her ring finger. "You're mine now, *bellissima*. There's no going back."

"I don't want to go back."

Their hunger knew no bounds as they began devouring each other all over again. Later when his cell phone rang, he groaned. It was probably the service. He hadn't called his patients yet.

"You need to get that," she whispered against his lips.

"I'm afraid I do." Nico eased himself away from her and stood up before answering it. He was still trembling with desire for her.

She got to her feet on those elegant legs of hers. While he was on the phone, she took the sack of food into the kitchen and warmed everything up in the microwave.

He stood in the doorway watching her every movement as he returned calls to patients. Talk about a vision in white and gold.

By the time he'd finished, she'd put their food on the table. The aroma of the coffee she'd made reminded him he was starving. Nico kissed her succulent lips before sitting down with her to eat. "How come I'm so lucky?"

"I've been asking myself that question since the evening you asked if you could drive me home from the hospital. My feet don't touch the ground anymore."

"I know the feeling."

When they'd finished eating, he reached for her hand and pulled her up against him. "Nothing's changed since last night." He smothered her with kisses. "I want you in my bed, so I'm thinking we should get married now. When the time comes to decide the course of my life, I want us to be man and wife already so we can make the decision together. I've found I don't want to do anything without you."

She moaned against his mouth. "I feel the same way. But that would mean going through a ceremony right away."

"That's the whole idea. How does tomorrow sound? I don't need anyone's permission. Naturally I'd like your parents' blessing. Shall we call them now and tell them our plans?"

He heard her sharp intake of breath. "*Nico*—be serious!"

"You think I'm not?"

"But getting married that fast would be impossible!"

"Not so. Enzo will arrange it."

"How?"

"As *duca* of Piedmont, he has magistrate power to waive the rules and ask the priest to marry us in the *castello* chapel. He's done it for several others on a moment's notice. Once our marriage is a fait accompli, we won't have to worry if word gets out that we're expecting our first child. What do you say?"

She clung to him, staring into his eyes with a hint of anxiety.

He kissed the end of her nose. "Now who's afraid."

"If I'm afraid, it has to do with your future. Everything's up in the air where the queen is concerned. If we're going to do this, don't you think you need to let her know?"

Nico rubbed his hands up and down her silky arms. "Where the love of my life is concerned, it's no one else's business. Protocol be damned! Are you ready to take the plunge with me, *tesora*? Yes or no."

By the way her eyes lit up, he could tell she was excited at the thought. "You honestly believe Enzo can arrange everything by tomorrow?"

"All I have to do is get him on the phone. The decision is yours. What about your parents?"

Fausta looked dazed. "I think it would be better if we call them after we say our vows."

"Are you sure? I don't want you to do something that could sever your relationship with them forever."

"It won't."

"You don't know that."

"My parents will be overjoyed when they learn that I married the son of King Carlo."

"But you'll be denying them the pleasure of watching the ceremony."

She chuckled. "I'd rather avoid the pomp. Think of the money that could be used for a good cause, like the other wing of the veterans' hospital. Honestly I know my parents will be so happy I married a prince, they'll get over it."

"Even if I'm illegitimate?"

"That won't worry my parents. If they had known you'd been available all these years, I can promise that *you* would have been the first name on their short list."

A burst of laughter poured out of Nico. *Happy* didn't begin to describe what he was feeling. It killed him to let her go, but he had to. "In that case I'll walk you out to your car in plain sight of our bodyguards."

They left the apartment. When they reached the car she'd parked on the street, she turned to him. "Aren't you going to give me one last kiss?" He'd already opened the door for her.

"I don't dare. Looking the way you do right now, it's a miracle I'm letting you go. Starting tomorrow, life will be a different story morning, noon and night."

Heat suffused her face. "How can you be away from the hospital again?"

"Let me worry about that. Be ready at six in the morning when I come by for you, *bellissima*. Wear casual clothes. By afternoon I'll deliver you back to the palace and the bodyguards will think I was paying a house call on Enzo and Pippa. I'll take my doctor bag with me. No one will know anything happened. It'll be our secret, at least for a while."

Her eyes swam with tears. "I love you so terribly, Nico, I don't want to leave you."

He felt her love to the marrow. "We badly need to be married, Fausta." He blew her a kiss and shut the door. After she drove off, he returned to his apartment and phoned his receptionist at home.

Nico told her he wouldn't be coming in until one tomorrow. He asked her to move the morning appointments to the afternoon schedule and he'd fit everyone in somehow. Then he got on the phone with Enzo.

"Nicolo—what's going on?"

"How are you feeling?"

"Never been better."

"That's good because I'm getting married

tomorrow morning and need the help only you can provide if you grasp my meaning."

The older man laughed. "I'm glad to hear you took Pippa's advice. As for mine…"

"I'm in love and can't wait, Enzo."

"Obviously Fausta can't either. I'd better get on the phone to the priest. How soon can we expect you?"

"We'll arrive at the *castello* at eight a.m. Can you arrange for the priest to meet us in the chapel for a quick ceremony? You and Pippa will be our witnesses. When we've said our vows, we'll have to get right back to Domodossola so no one suspects anything, not even Fausta's parents. That was her decision, not mine."

"Sounds like her. That girl knows what she wants. What I want to know is, how long do you expect your marriage to remain a secret?"

"Only until she tells her parents. But the point is, I decided to take your sage advice about weighing my decision. That's why I want Fausta to be my wife first. Together we'll choose whether to stay in Domodossola or leave for La Valazzura when the time comes."

"Bravo, figlio mio."

"Once again you're saving my life, Enzo."

"You saved mine the day I interviewed you at the farm. Pippa and I decided you'd been sent to us in our grandson's place."

Nico's throat swelled with so much emotion he couldn't talk.

"It will be our joy to see you married to the adorable Fausta. Knowing what I do about her, she'll make the kind of loving companion Pippa has always been to me."

When Nico could find the words, he said, "I couldn't ask for more than that. *Ci vediamo domani.*"

At five to six the next morning, Fausta came out of the palace doors carrying her purse. Nico was already there. She climbed in his car, wearing jeans and a soft pink cotton top with short sleeves. His piercing dark eyes devoured her before he drove away. "How did you sleep?"

"I've been so excited, I couldn't."

"You look fabulous anyway."

She laughed. "Thank you. I'm glad you like my wedding dress. It's a Fausta original."

A grin broke out on his handsome face. "I've got food and coffee in the back seat when you're ready to eat."

"Goody! I'm hungry now. I'll feed both of us."

"I was hoping you'd say that."

Fausta reached around and put the sack and thermos in her lap. "You're going to make the most satisfactory husband on earth."

"Tell me that again in fifty years and I'll believe you." His gaze darted to her hand. "Where's your ring?"

"In my purse."

"I'll need it to put on your finger during the ceremony."

A small moan escaped. "I don't have one for you yet. I wanted to ask Lanza for help but didn't dare." She took it out of her purse. He put it in his breast pocket.

"Don't worry. Enzo will find something for you to give me."

Fausta poured coffee in the cup and handed it to him. She couldn't stop staring at her breathtaking fiancé. He smelled wonderful as always. Today he wore a tan jacket covering a button-up white shirt and dark trousers.

"What did Enzo say when you called him?"

"He and Pippa are overjoyed with our news."

"They don't think we're crazy?"

He smiled. "I didn't say that, but they're happy for us."

"I hope he doesn't tell Lorenzo."

"He won't, but let's not forget you came to my apartment last evening. Your parents couldn't be happy about it since it was your second visit to enemy territory. This evening after work you'll be driving to my apartment again. I wouldn't be surprised if they send security to my door."

Fausta handed him a ham-filled croissant and took one for herself. "Then we'll phone the parents tonight and give them our glorious news. That is if our bodyguards haven't caught on to our devious scheme before then."

"Who knows?" After they'd eaten, he put a hand on her arm. "Any regrets?"

Her crystalline blue eyes clouded over. "How can you even ask me that? I'm so in love with you, it's indecent."

"That makes two of us. Do you know when I saw you in the cafeteria with Mia, I thought you were a celebrity because you seemed familiar? Your beauty, everything about you drew me in. The next time I saw you in Tommaso's room, I couldn't believe my eyes.

"But when he called you Fausta, my heart almost failed me because it was then I realized you were Princess Rossiano. By the time I'd recovered my wits, you'd left too fast for me to be able to catch up to you. I was haunted by you until your next visit to the ward. At that point I'd lain in wait for you. No way was I going to let you get away from me again."

The intensity of his deep voice found its way to the deepest recesses of her soul.

"I didn't want to get away. You were the most amazing man to come into my life. When you turned down my invitation to come to my apartment, I told Mia I'd made a huge mistake with you."

"You know that's not true."

"I do now, but that night I was afraid I didn't measure up to you. I worried that you didn't find me interesting enough. Let's be honest. In many ways I've led a sheltered life compared to yours. More than ever I hated it that I was a royal. I feared that you wouldn't be back. The torture I went through." She shook her head.

"You didn't witness the torture I went

through. While we ate at Prospero's *cantina*, I sat there thinking that I'd met the woman of my desire. No other woman had ever come close or ever would. Prospero's eyes lit up to see that the princess of the realm had honored him by eating at his restaurant.

"For that night you were *my* princess. I was the happiest man alive until I drove you back to the palace that represented the dividing line between us. For a time I'd forgotten. When you asked me inside—"

"Every lesson Angelo had tried to teach you got in the way," Fausta broke in. "I didn't know how to fight it."

"You didn't have to. You already had me hooked body and soul, and now you're about to become my wife. Whatever happens, wherever we end up, I swear I'll love you forever, Fausta."

Too touched by his words, all she could do was clutch his hand for the rest of the drive to the *castello*.

After they arrived and Nico had parked the car in the courtyard, he grabbed his doctor bag and opened Fausta's door. Enzo, looking sporty, was waiting for them at the entrance with a huge smile on his face. He hugged Nico before turning to her.

"You're right on time for your own wedding. *Congratulazioni*, Fausta." He gave her a warm hug, which she reciprocated. "Nico says you're on a tight time schedule, so the priest has been warned. Since I'm taking your father's place to give you away, I'll walk you to the chapel where Pippa is waiting."

"Thank you so much, Enzo."

"It's an honor."

Nico left the bag in the foyer and they proceeded to walk down several hallways of portraits and tapestries to the small chapel on the main floor. With candles lit, the interior dazzled the eye like a jewel. Fausta adored everything, including the beautiful statues, but she didn't see the priest yet.

Pippa sat in her wheelchair near the altar. While Enzo took Nico aside, she tugged on Fausta's hands and pulled her down to kiss her cheek. "You're marrying a veritable prince, but you already know that."

She nodded. "He's the prince of my heart."

"You've caught the eye of a most amazing and wonderful man. I know you're both going to be very happy."

"Dear Pippa—*grazie* for arranging this for us."

"We wondered if we would ever see this day. Nicolo seemed so determined to find his parents, I feared he would never find true love. Then he brought you inside the *castello*. The look in your eyes told me everything I wanted to know."

Fausta struggled for breath. "He's my life."

Pippa handed her a man's gold band. "This is the wedding ring I gave Enzo. He wants you to give it to Nico for the ceremony."

"I can't take this."

"Yes, you can. It means the world to my husband. He loves Nico like a son."

"You two are so dear."

As she put it in her blouse pocket, the priest walked in. He was young and quite handsome. No doubt he was surprised she was wearing pants. Not even a veil.

"Father Pietro, allow me to introduce Princess Fausta Rossiano of Domodossola."

"*Principessa*. I understand this must be a secret, quick ceremony. I'll do my best."

"You're very kind to perform the service, let alone this early in the morning. We're indebted to you."

Enzo and Nico moved toward them. "Father? I'd like you to meet Dr. Nico Barsotti. How do you wish to proceed?"

"If you'll sit by your wife, I'll ask these two to stand in front of me. Dr. Barsotti, if you'll take the right hand of Princess Rossiano?"

Fausta could hardly believe this was really happening. Nico gripped her hand, holding it fast, but her heart was pounding much faster.

CHAPTER TEN

"DEARLY BELOVED, Nico and Fausta. Marriage is the most important of all earthly relationships. It should be entered into reverently, thoughtfully and with full understanding of its sacred nature. Your marriage must stand by the strength of your love and the power of faith in each other and in God."

Fausta believed that to the core of her soul.

"Love is very patient and kind, never jealous or envious, never boastful or proud. Love is never haughty, rude or selfish."

Except that she'd been selfish, but never again.

"Love does not demand its own way. Love is never glad about injustice but rejoices whenever truth wins out."

Truth had finally won out and Nico now had full knowledge of his parentage. Fausta knew the news he'd waited for a lifetime had released him and had made him free.

"If you love someone," the priest spoke on, "you will be loyal to them no matter the cost. You will always believe in them, always expect the best in them and will always stand your ground in defending them."

Those were vows she would defend with her life.

The priest eyed Nico. "Knowing what is expected, do you, Nico, take Fausta to be your lawfully wedded wife?"

Nico answered in his deep voice, "I do."

At that point the priest looked at Fausta. "Knowing what is expected, do you, Fausta, take Nico to be your lawfully wedded husband?"

"I do with all my heart," she avowed.

A small smile broke out on the priest's face. "You will now exchange rings."

Fausta met Nico's glance before they reached in their pockets. He put the diamond ring back on her finger and squeezed her hand. She followed by placing Enzo's ring on Nico's finger with trembling hands. He had to have been surprised but didn't let it show.

"In as much as you have given each other

these tokens of abiding love in the sight of witnesses, then by the power invested in me by the Church, I pronounce you man and wife. What God has joined together, let no man put asunder."

He blessed them. "In the name of the Father, the Son and the Holy Spirit. Amen. You may kiss your bride."

The short, almost surreal yet perfect ceremony had come to an end.

She was so insanely happy she raised her head to Nico, whose eyes burned with desire for her. He pulled her closer and gave her a husband's possessive kiss, thrilling her in every part of her being. Fausta clung to his hard, fit body, giving him everything she possessed to show him what he meant to her.

"Every dream of mine has come true," he whispered before drowning her in passion that filled her with indescribable rapture. "We have two hours before we have to drive home. Come with me."

Blind with love, she went where he took her. They left the chapel and ascended the staircase to an apartment on the second floor. After picking her up in his arms, he carried her through to the bedroom and followed her down on the bed.

"Mia moglie—" Nico cried against her mouth.

She really was his wife now! They couldn't get close enough fast enough. No kiss lasted long enough.

"It should be a sin how beautiful you are. Love me, Fausta."

"That's all I've ever wanted to do since I first laid eyes on you, *amore mio*. Don't ever stop loving me."

"As if I could."

The divine sensation of lying in his arms for the next two hours and knowing his possession sent her into ecstasy. Fausta had been able to only imagine what it would be like to know her husband's possession. But her imagination hadn't given her a clue of what really went on with this incredible man, who made her feel loved and immortal.

They groaned in breathless protest when the house phone rang. Nico didn't pick up. They both knew it was Enzo reminding them they needed to leave for Domodossola if Nico wanted to keep his afternoon appointments at the hospital.

"We need to get up," she whispered against his lips, but she couldn't bear to move out of his arms.

"Not yet, *squisita*." His mouth kissed every feature of her face as a prelude to making love all over again. But when the phone rang a second time, they both knew what it meant.

Fausta slid out of bed, provoking another groan from him, and hurried to the bathroom to shower and dress. Nico followed suit before engulfing her in one long kiss in the doorway before they left the bedroom. "This will have to last until tonight."

Together they flew down the staircase to the salon where their two favorite people were seated. While Nico removed the ring and handed it back to Enzo, Fausta put the diamond ring back in her pocket. They all hugged.

"You'll never know what you've done for us. This is the happiest day of our lives," Fausta told them.

Pippa beamed. "To see you two this deliriously in love is pure joy for us. I have a gift for you. Open it when you get home."

"You shouldn't have."

"When you open it, you won't feel that way."

Fausta kissed her again and put the small sealed sack in her purse. "I'm embarrassed we didn't get to say goodbye to Father Pietro. Please tell him how much we appreciated his doing the service for us. We'll send him a note and be in touch with you soon."

After signing all the marriage documents, they rushed out to the car. Enzo brought Nico the doctor bag and saw them off, smiling at both of them. "You lucky people. I envy you. Let the adventure begin."

After starting the car and driving out of the courtyard, Nico reached for her hand. "We're on an adventure all right," he declared. "I'll never forget this day or the fact that Enzo let you put his wedding ring on my finger."

"He loves you like a son."

She heard him suck in his breath. "He and Pippa made it possible for us to become man and wife today. Are you happy, Signora Barsotti?"

"I think you know the answer to that. Do you have any idea how much I love the sound of my new name?" she cried emotionally. "I wish—"

"I know," he broke in. "The last thing I wanted to do was leave the *castello*. We need weeks and weeks to be alone together. I'm in more agony now than ever before and would never suggest putting a two hour time limit on the wedding night."

"No." She squeezed his hand hard.

His car ate up the miles as they sped back to Domodossola. He darted her a glance. "We need all night tonight. After work I'll come straight to the apartment."

"You'll probably be late seeing patients. I'll need a key so I can bring some of my things over early and have dinner waiting."

"I'm not sure I'll be able to eat. One sight of you and everything else will go out of my head except to take you in my arms."

"I don't honestly know how I'm going to wait long enough for you to come home."

"Tell me about it."

As he drove over the speed limit, she looked at her watch. They were nearing the city. "If you're supposed to be at the hospital at one, then don't drive me to the palace. That'll take too much time. I'll go inside with you and call for the limo. It'll look more natural since I've often gone there to meet with Mia."

"Are you going to tell her about us?"

"I won't say anything to anyone until you and I feel it's right."

"Your parents must be told first."

"Agreed. We'll talk about it tonight."

Before long he pulled into the physicians' parking lot and parked in his spot. Fausta got out on her own and walked inside the hospital behind him. Once inside the doors, he pulled a key off his key chain and handed it to her.

Their gazes fused with longing. "Until tonight, *tesora*."

While he walked away, she put the key in her purse and pulled out her cell phone. In a few minutes the limo pulled up to the entrance. The driver opened the rear door for her.

Fausta climbed in, secretly overjoyed that she was now Dr. Barsotti's wife. Was she ever! Visions of what had happened a couple of hours ago when he'd taken her to another realm of existence robbed her of breath. If the bodyguards following them knew about the marriage already, it didn't matter.

She put her head back and closed her eyes, dreaming of the night to come. If Nico's mother had been this in love with his father, Fausta couldn't imagine the pain they would have gone through to say goodbye.

Thank heaven Fausta didn't have to face a

permanent separation from Nico. They were husband and wife forever. As the priest had said, "What God has joined together, let no man put asunder."

Nico was just leaving his office at seven thirty p.m. after a packed schedule when Felipe showed up at the door. The two men gave each other a hug.

"I'm glad to see you back, *amico*. Let's get together. Want to go out for a beer right now? I want to tell you about my wedding plans."

Stifling a moan, Nico said, "There's nothing I'd like more, but I have to go out on an emergency house call. Can we do it tomorrow night? Five thirtyish? I won't let anything get in the way." He hated lying to his buddy, but he had no choice.

"Sure. You have a sick patient?"

"Very sick." *I'm the patient and need to get back to Fausta or I'm not going to make it.*

"Then I won't keep you. Until tomorrow night!"

Nico patted his friend's arm and dashed for the stairs. A whole evening and night to make love to his wife. Was there ever a more beautiful woman alive, inside and out, or one more loving?

He drove to his apartment and parked the car, eager to get her to himself. She'd left the door unlocked. Something smelled delicious. After hurrying inside, he found her in the kitchen by the stove wearing a white lace negligee that caused him to gasp.

"What took you so long?" She flashed him a seductive smile that melted his insides. "Our dinner is ready to be eaten. Why don't you freshen up and then join me at the table for our first meal together as a wedded couple." She'd set it with glasses of red wine and a vase of white roses.

He could hardly think, let alone make a sound. Finally, he managed, "I'll be right back." A quick trip to the bedroom to change into his robe and wash his hands, he returned to the kitchen.

"Sit down, *amato*, and open your gift first."

In a daze, he unwrapped the tiny box by his glass and pulled out a man's gold band. "We'll get it inscribed later. Try it on and see if it fits."

His heart thudded. "I need your help."

"No, you don't, or this roast pig from Prospero's will go to waste."

Fausta...

"I guess we can't have that." He put it on.

"You're mine now and I'll adore you forever."

Forever.

She put their dinner plates full of food on the table and sat down. While he was trying to take in her beauty and all that she'd created here, she lifted her wineglass. The blue diamond ring was back on her finger. "To the husband who has made me thankful I was born." There were tears in her voice.

Nico lifted his glass. "To the wife who made an orphan feel like a king and has literally transformed my life."

He clinked her glass and they drank the liquid, which glistened on her lips, reminding him of the first time at the *cantina*. He would have sold his soul to kiss her that night. Tonight he intended to kiss the two of them into oblivion.

Her eyes feasted on him as they ate. "Roast pig has become my favorite meal. Every step of your life has enamored me. I guess you saw Pippa give me a gift before we left the *castello*. They were little photographs of you taken from the time you were twelve. I studied them for hours."

He took a quick breath. "Trust Pippa."

"You have no idea how precious they are to me, but she knew what they would mean to me. What a darling boy you were! No wonder you captured their hearts. I'm going to have each one framed." She stared into his eyes. "Tonight, I'm putting in an order for a baby who looks just like you."

"I already put in one earlier today, for an enchanting princess with hair of gold and jewel blue eyes, but I'm more than eager to accommodate you this very minute." He got up from the table and pulled her after him.

Nico could see she'd already inhabited his bedroom. Her feminine items draped around had turned his apartment into a love nest. Giorgio had come out of the closet and sat on the chair. Overcome with emotion, he crushed her to him. He'd never imagined happiness like this was possible.

"I need you, *squisita*—I want to love you and never let you go." In the next breath they lay down together. Throughout the hours of the night they gave in to the passion consuming them. His ardent lover thrilled him.

Enzo had called her adorable. Fausta was that, and so many other things—he was blown away by her womanly magic.

He would never be able to get enough of
her. Toward morning they both fell asleep
with their legs entangled, her face burrowed
against his shoulder.

When he heard a phone ring, he knew he
couldn't ignore it. A patient might be calling
who needed him. But Fausta was one step
ahead of him.

"It's my phone, Nico. I'll get it. You sleep."
She reached for it on the bedside table, but
by now he was awake. For someone to call
her at five thirty in the morning concerned
him.

She sat up to talk. All he heard her say
was "Lanza." After a minute, she thanked
her and hung up.

"What's going on, Fausta?"

"I think you can guess." She put the phone
on the table and returned to his arms.

"So, our secret is out."

"Yes. My bodyguards saw us go in with
your doctor's bag. Then they saw the priest
leave the *castello* and knew something was
wrong. They caught up to the priest and
said they were on the king's business. He
told them he'd performed a marriage service for you and me. That's all they needed
to hear.

"Lanza wanted to give us a heads-up that the parents are now in the know. They wanted to find out what she knew. I'm glad she couldn't tell them anything."

"So am I, Fausta, but we need to talk to them before I have to leave for the office. My first appointment is at nine. Let's get dressed right now and drive to the palace. What we need to tell them has to be said face-to-face. They deserve to know every-thing. I want them to know how much I love you."

She threw her arms around his neck. "It's going to be all right, Nico. I promise."

"I'm not worried about me, *tesoro*. It's you."

"Don't worry about me. I have *you*."

Her faith in him was humbling. He re-called a certain conversation with Felipe.

I'm thankful I'm not in your shoes. When the time comes, I don't envy you. But for what it's worth, I defy the king to find a bet-ter man for his daughter than you.

"Mamma? Papa? I'd like to introduce you to my husband, Dr. Nico Barsotti, who is a family practice physician at the Hospital of the Three Crosses."

Fausta's parents had been waiting for them in the salon following her phone call to them.

Nico bowed with infinite composure. "Your Majesties. It's a great honor to meet you at last." With his tall, rock-solid build and dark hair, he looked fabulous in his tan suit and tie. She loved him so terribly, her heart hurt.

"How do you do, Dr. Barsotti." Her patrician father and mother made imposing figures, but she could always count on them to be kind. They'd faced difficult situations with her sisters' marriages. "Why don't you and Fausta be seated."

"Thank you."

She reached for Nico's hand and they sat on the love seat opposite her parents.

"Lanza phoned us at Nico's apartment earlier this morning. We imagined the news would leak out but hoped to have a chance to tell you before you heard it from anyone else. Since it's too late for that, we want you to know why we didn't come to you before now. Nico has an amazing story to tell. I'm going to let him explain."

Fausta's beloved husband sat forward and began his incredible tale, starting with life at the orphanage. As the revelations continued to unfold, she watched her parents' somber expressions change to ones of disbelief and eventual awe.

Her father was the first to shake his head. "You're the son of King Carlo and definitely look like him. How amazing, and how sad that you didn't get to meet him."

"As Signor Bruno explained, he didn't dare bring me out of hiding until he felt there was no threat."

"Your father was a remarkable king who had to rule under the very difficult circumstances of war. I would have attended his funeral if I'd been physically able."

Her mother had put a hand over her heart. "You never got to meet your mother either. I'm so sorry."

"So am I. Where the queen is concerned, I don't know what's going to happen. Fausta and I wanted to be married before I have to make a decision, but we just don't know what that decision will be until she reaches out to me."

Fausta felt her father's eyes on her. They were smiling. "You always knew your own mind. Are you still angry with me that I sent

Dego and his sister to school in Italy years ago?"

"Funny you would ask me that, Papa. Last night as I was getting our dinner ready at the apartment, I found myself thanking you for preserving me for Nico. He's my life." Her voice shook.

"That's the way it should be, *figlia mia*."

"I truly did want both of you at the ceremony, but the fuss of a royal wedding isn't for me. I know a worthy cause where we could donate the money."

Her father nodded. "I'm grateful for Enzo and Pippa."

"So are we!" she cried. "They were wonderful to help arrange for the priest to marry us."

Nico nodded. "They've been like parents to me. I owe them so much I can never repay them. Perhaps the day will come when you'll forgive us for getting married in private."

"That was my fault," Fausta blurted. "Nico wanted to tell you, but—"

"But you wanted to do it your own way," her mother said with a smile. "You always did, and now you've married the man who has set you on fire. We couldn't be happier.

Welcome to the family, Nico. Whether doctor or king, you've made our daughter happier than we've ever seen her."

"I'm the one who's happy. Fausta is a gift, one I'll treasure all the days of my life."

Fausta got to her feet. "I wish we could talk longer, but Nico has to get to the hospital."

Her parents stood up and walked over to Nico to give him a hug. It thrilled Fausta's heart to watch the three of them embrace.

"Walk me out," Nico whispered a minute later against her neck. When they reached the foyer, he gripped her upper arms tightly. "I never met such gracious people in my life."

"I told you it would be all right."

"No wonder you're the way you are. Thank heaven your father got rid of Dego. Thank heaven for Angelo. Thank heaven for Enzo and Pippa. Thank heaven for Lorenzo, who got me a position at the hospital. The day I met you was the beginning of my life, Fausta."

"And mine. What time can I expect you home?"

"I promised Felipe I'd go out for a beer with him after work. He wants to tell me about their wedding plans. Expect me by seven."

"After you tell him we're married, maybe you might make it by eight?" she teased and pressed a kiss to his lips. "I won't be able to breathe till you get home."

Later that evening Felipe came in to Nico's office at quarter to six. They left in their cars for a favorite pub that served sandwiches and local beer. After ordering from the bar, they found a booth. Sports reviews were on the TV closest to them.

They talked about Felipe's wedding set for August 5. There would be a rehearsal dinner the night before.

Nico was about to tell Felipe everything when there was a news flash that interrupted the latest scores of soccer matches.

"We interrupt this program to bring you breaking news from the royal palace. In a secret wedding ceremony, twenty-five-year-old Princess Fausta Rossiano, middle daughter of King Victor and Queen Ginata, was recently married to commoner Dr. Nico Barsotti. More details will be forthcoming on the ten o'clock news. Now back to our regularly scheduled program."

Felipe let out a whoop everyone in the pub could hear. A grin broke out on his face. "You sly fox. I knew something's been going on. How come I had to hear it on the news?"

Nico lowered his beer glass. "You would have been the first person I told, but Fausta and I still hadn't talked to her parents and that didn't happen until this morning at the palace. I'm positive they didn't release this news to the press, so of course there's been a leak." Which meant Basil and Queen Liliane had heard about it too.

"Where did you get married? When?"

In the next little while Nico told him everything. His friend studied him in sheer amazement as his story unfolded.

"*Santo cielo!* Over the years you've been looking for your parents, when all this time you've been the son of King Carlo? And now you're the heir apparent to the throne of La Valazzura? This is the most incredible thing I ever heard."

Nico nodded. "I'm still trying to deal with it. If I didn't have Fausta with me…" He finished the rest of his beer. "Nothing's final. It can't be until I hear from the queen. My father's evil cousin, Giuseppe Umberto, wants the throne for himself. A battle is waging for control over there."

"Would you hate me if I said I hope you stay in Domodossola for the rest of your lives? Mia adores Fausta. It'll be a loss neither of us will get over."

Those words warmed Nico. "How could I hate you when you've been the closest thing I'll ever have to a brother?"

"Amen."

"I love being a doctor, Felipe. I'm not sure I can give it up." He let out a troubled sigh. "But whatever happens, I promise you we'll be here for your wedding. It'll be my privilege to be your best man."

"Is it all right if I tell Mia?"

"She's probably heard already."

"But not *your* story. I'm sure you want to get back to Fausta. You're still on your honeymoon. Let's go."

After another hug, they parted company at their cars. Nico drove home knowing Fausta was there waiting for him. She was all he could think about as he hurried inside the apartment, breathless to sweep her in his arms.

He thought he'd find her in the bedroom since he'd returned later than he'd meant to.

Instead he saw her sitting in the living room still dressed in casual clothes. His normally radiant wife looked worried. She wasn't alone. Signor Bruno was with her.

La Valazzura's intelligence agents worked with a speed that didn't escape Nico.

CHAPTER ELEVEN

"Basil?" He walked over and shook his hand, then sat next to Fausta and grasped her hand. "I take it you've heard the news about our wedding."

The older man nodded. "What's more important, the queen has her spies and your marriage has caused such a serious problem for her, she has sent me here to talk to you personally. Perhaps your wife should be the one to explain to you since I've told her everything."

Nico turned to her. "What's going on, *tesoro*?"

"The queen made the decision that she wants you to be the next king. Since she's Slovenian, she has a young cousin, Princess Anne of Slovenia, who will make you the perfect wife. A marriage between the two of you will keep the ties close between your two countries. Therefore, she wants our marriage dissolved as if it had never been.

"For the sake of the crown you should listen to him, Nico. I'm an impediment. We've only been married for two days and could end it just as quickly."

Angrier than he'd ever been in his life, Nico got to his feet. "When I met with her, Basil, I was a single man. We didn't discuss my marital state, nor did she lay down any conditions."

"Nevertheless, she has now set the rules. I'm here to present them to you."

"Do you mean to tell me that even though she knows I've just married my heart's desire, she could cold-bloodedly ask me to divorce my new wife in order to gain the throne?"

Basil stood up, composed as ever. "She knows your chances could fail if you arrive with a foreign-born wife. It could create more problems for our paranoid nation. She fears the parliament would have great difficulty accepting the situation or trusting it."

Nico didn't believe any of these reasons were the major force driving the queen. She was still unforgiving of what Nico's father had done to her. But it would give her some satisfaction to know he would have to take a new bride he didn't love in order to fill his father's shoes. Somehow, she would have her revenge if he divorced Fausta.

His body tautened. "Thank you for delivering her message to me. You can return to La Valazzura and tell her that no earthly throne is more important to me than a celestial marriage. I plan to live with Fausta through eternity."

Basil's eyes studied him for a long moment. "You'd make a remarkable king. Your cousin will never be able to fill your father's shoes, but I know you could."

"Thank you for the vote of confidence, Basil."

The cousin of Nico's father was banging on the doors of the Azzura palace, ready to burst them down. Let him.

"Thank you for being so gracious, Princess."

As Basil had discovered, Fausta was the epitome of all those exceptional Rossiano qualities. Nico had never loved her more than he did at this moment.

"I'll convey your decision to the queen." Their visitor bowed to both of them and left the apartment.

"Bellissima—" He swung around to embrace her, but she stood at a distance, all closed up. Nico knew that look. "The waiting is over, *grazie a Dio.* Our new life is ahead of us. Come to bed with me. I'm aching for you."

She took another step back. "We have to talk first."

He took a deep breath. "There's nothing to talk about. We're staying here in Domodossola for the rest of our lives."

"Nico—you've just been told that Queen Liliane wants you to be the new ruler of your country and take over where your father left off. We know it's what he would have wanted if he were still alive."

"Except that she wasn't honest with me and had her own secret agenda. I'm a married man now and that disqualifies me."

"But we can get a divorce."

His brows furrowed. "I'm going to pretend I didn't hear you say that."

"You have to listen to me! You've been on a path your entire life to discover your identity. I believe with all my heart that you're supposed to be the new king. There've been too many little miracles along the way that prove to me you're the one who's been destined to be the head of the country."

Her words gutted him. "Does our love mean so little to you that one word from the queen and you're willing to destroy everything between us so that I can be king?"

"No. I'm not saying this right. Please, darling, I—"

"I think you are," he cut her off. "Is it possible that my becoming king at any cost is more important to you than I am? How many times have we talked about the class difference between us? I'm beginning to see that there truly is a gigantic gulf that separates our thinking."

She shook her head. At this point tears were spilling down her pale cheeks. "I need to explain what I meant."

"I heard you loud and clear. You're from the aristocracy. You people really do march to a holy drum. Angelo was right. Queen Liliane has decreed what she deems necessary, and you fall on your sword. But where does that leave me? According to you, there is no *us*! Our wedding ceremony can be discarded for the greater good. Is that it?"

"Yes!" she cried. "Because you're a magnificent man, one who's destined for greater things than most men on this earth. It's your birthright! You heard Basil. I saw the way he looked and spoke to you. He holds you in reverence and you can't deny it."

"I deny nothing. But I'm beginning to wonder how you can consider making such a sacrifice, *unless* our love pales in comparison to the love you had for Dego. Is that what this is about? This morning your father asked if you'd forgiven him for sending Dego away. I find it amazing that after all this time, his name was still brought up. Is *he* the one you'll never be able to forget? Is that why you're able to consider letting me go?"

"No, darling. You have this all wrong."

He headed for the bedroom. "Nothing you could say is going to take away my pain. Drive safely when you go home."

She followed him. "I'm not leaving. This is my home."

"I don't think so. We might not have signed papers yet, but I already feel divorced."

"Don't you know I only said these things because I don't want to be the one who holds you back from your real purpose in life?"

He wheeled around. "I thought we were going to make all our decisions together! I'm not at all certain what my real purpose in life is except to be your husband and the father of our children! I thought that was what you wanted."

"*It is*, or I wouldn't be your wife right now. But, Nico, I was with you that day we drove to Biella and visited the orphanage. You revealed the secrets of your heart to me. I visited with those who loved you. You're a unique man who has gifts the world needs."

"Needs my own wife can give up for the whim of the queen?"

"How can you say it's a whim?"

"She found a way to get back at my father by making a decision she knew would tear me apart. But the only person who has torn me apart is you. I'm going out for a while, but I'll be back."

"Please don't leave—"

"Just give me a little time."

He heard her call his name, but his pain was too deep, and he kept walking.

Nico, Nico. At two thirty in the morning he still hadn't come home. Beyond sick, Fausta paced the floor. When she heard the ding on her phone she checked the text message.

I've gone to the office. Won't be home until after work.

This was a Nico she didn't recognize. She'd done this to him.

Beyond tears, she lay awake until midmorning, soul-searching. As she sorted through their conversation, it stunned her that he thought she still loved Dego. He couldn't be jealous of him!

But the more she dug for answers, the more she understood that the orphan boy hadn't owned anything of his own. He didn't want to belong to anyone but his own parents. Everything he'd received while growing up had been given to him by well-meaning strangers. He didn't have anything of his own until he'd earned his first paycheck as a doctor. Even then he sent money to Angelo.

All his life had been a fight to compete and survive. Then he'd met her, and another kind of fight had ensued. He'd overcome the great obstacle in his mind to marry her knowing she was royal. Yet no sooner had they gotten married than Basil had shown up with the queen's proposition. And what had Fausta done?

She'd flung Nico's love for her in his face when it was the last thing she'd ever meant to do. To tell him she'd give him a divorce after the two days of joy they'd just shared was so cruel, she couldn't believe she'd said it. Fausta needed to repair the damage before any more time passed.

The first thing she did was call his work. His receptionist answered. "Dr. Barsotti's office."

"Hello? My name is Eugenia Santi. This is an emergency. Could the doctor see me at the end of the day? It's a female problem that's getting much worse."

"Are you bleeding?"

"No, but the pain is severe."

"I see. Has he seen you before?"

"Yes, but it was a house call."

"He has another late patient too, but why don't you come at five thirty p.m. and I'll see if he'll fit you in after that. Otherwise you may have to go to the ER."

"Thank you."

The second she hung up, she showered and washed her hair. Then she put on a filmy dress in a blue and yellow print with flutter sleeves. With blue forget-me-not earrings and a splash of her favorite fragrance, she felt ready to take on her unsuspecting husband.

Her heart was thudding so hard she was

afraid the patients waiting for him could hear it as she entered the reception room and reported to the receptionist. The woman stared hard at her. "I'm afraid it's going to be a wait, Signora Santi." She'd noticed the blue diamond ring Fausta was wearing.

"It doesn't matter as long as I get to see him."

After an hour the receptionist told her she could go in. This was a whole new experience for Fausta, who'd never visited him here. Her excitement was off the charts when she entered his impressive-looking booklined office.

He wore a white lab coat and had been putting something into the computer. When he turned to her, the look on his face was worth all the trouble she'd gone to to surprise him. His eyes devoured her inch by inch.

"I told your receptionist I was having female problems," she began before he could say a word. "But I lied because it's a heart problem. The worst kind there is, and it's so painful no pill or operation can fix it. You see, it's my husband. I hurt him so terribly, I don't know how to win him back. At this point my pain is unbearable.

"Please tell me you can help me. Maybe

if I explain, you can give me some advice. You see, he has had to fight for everything all his life. He fought for me against all odds. But when it was my turn to fight for him, I told him I wouldn't stand in his way if he wanted something more. It was the wrong thing to say. All he wanted was me and he has proven it over and over again.

"*Dottore?* How do I prove that all I want in this life is his love? How do I convince him that what I once felt for a boy from childhood was simple puppy love? I didn't know the meaning of love until I met my husband. If I don't get help soon, I'm not going make it."

Nico's expression didn't change as he buzzed his receptionist and told her she could go home.

"If you'll step into the examining room, I'll listen to your heart and we'll go from there."

Holding her breath, she followed him into the other room.

"Let me help you sit on the table." He put his hands around her hips and lifted her with ease. Their bodies brushed together, sending a thrill through her. She waited breathlessly as he reached for his stethoscope and started listening to her heart. His jaw was pressed against her cheek. He smelled divine.

"You're right. A lot of damage has been done. It's pounding way too hard to be healthy. I want you to lie down."

Heat swept over her as she lay back. He slid his hands up her arms and pinned her there. His eyes were like lasers as he examined her features. "Your poor husband. You're so beautiful. He must have a heart attack every time he lets you out in public. My advice is that you go home and make love to him. Never let him go, not even after you've convinced him that you love him the way he loves you."

"I promise," she whispered. "Kiss me, Dr. Barsotti, or I think I'm going to pass out from wanting you too much."

"Well we can't have that. Not in my office."

His mouth found hers and he kissed her close to senseless. Tears beaded her lashes. Her husband had forgiven her. She couldn't ask for anything more.

"I have news, *bellissima*," he murmured. "This afternoon I had a phone call from Basil. After he reported to the queen, she said that she'd only been testing me to see if

I was an honorable man. If I hadn't passed the test, that would have been it. But because I loved you more than I loved anything else, she says she wants me to fly to La Valazzura with you.

"Basil told me she'd like to meet the woman who was prepared to put me first if that's what you wanted for me, even if it meant a divorce. With that kind of unselfish love, she feels you'll make the perfect queen. I guess I have some serious rethinking to do where the queen is concerned."

"Darling—the room is spinning. I really think I'm going to pass out."

"Keep holding on. Don't faint on me. We need to go home and talk about what we want to do. Our world is out there waiting, whichever one it is."

EPILOGUE

The small royal dining room of the palace had been lit with candles. A fragrance from the pink roses filled the ornate room. Fausta knew her mother had picked and arranged them for this delicious roast pig dinner to welcome Nico into the family. Jeanne, the head chef at the palace, had really outdone herself as a favor to Fausta to honor her new husband with his favorite meal.

Her parents sat at one end. Lanza and Donetta sat across from each other with their husbands. Fausta and Nico had found their places at the other end. Their family had sat around this table all their lives, but tonight everything was different for Fausta. For the first time since she was a little girl, she no longer felt conflicted about being royal and enjoyed a sense of belonging that was new to her.

Falling in love with Nico had changed her perspective on life. She knew a sense of completeness and was so full of joy she could hardly contain it.

Her father tapped his wine goblet with a spoon and got to his feet. "What a glorious sight! Our three precious daughters married to husbands they love and who love them. What father or mother could ask for more, especially when they are the finest men Ginata and I know."

Fausta smiled at her husband, who squeezed her thigh beneath the table.

"Nico—that's how we know you—welcome to the family," her father continued. "Whatever path you and Fausta choose to take, whether you remain Dr. Barsotti here in Domodossola, or Crown Prince Massimo in La Valazzura, we support you and wish you joy.

"Our Fausta followed her dream to marry a commoner. You got your wish, poppet. We got our wish too, because he makes you so happy. And…it doesn't hurt that he's the son of King Carlo, a sovereign I always admired."

While everyone chuckled, Fausta's eyes filled with tears.

"Ginata and I are content and looking forward to enjoying our Rufy and soon-to-be born grandchildren for years to come. Therefore, we've decided now is the time for me to give up the crown. It will be conferred on Stefano, who is Lanza's beloved and has been my rock since he joined the family.

"The coronation will take place in a week because Enrico must soon get back to Vallefiore to run the affairs of his kingdom. Before he and Donetta leave, we want our whole family together to sustain Stefano as the new king of Domodossola."

Everyone clapped for Stefano, who hugged Lanza.

When everyone had congratulated him, her father added, "If Nico decides to step in to his father's shoes, then we'll all fly to La Valazzura to see his coronation whether the doctor gives me permission or not."

"Papa!" the girls cried in fear.

Suddenly her mother stood up. "Don't worry. He may have been in charge all these years, but now that he's stepping down, it's my turn to lay down the law and I'm not letting him out of my sight! We're not going anywhere. If necessary, we'll watch Nico's coronation on television."

Fausta squeezed Nico's hand before hurrying to the other end of the table to hug her parents. Her sisters got there first.

When she finally turned around, she saw the husbands huddled in one corner of the dining room talking quietly. It thrilled her that Nico was already bonding with his brothers-in-law. As she approached, Nico saw her coming and started toward her. Talk about a blinding light of happiness. Like Fausta, her husband had found peace.

* * * * *